SAM CRESCENT

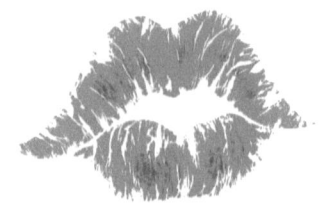

EVERNIGHT PUBLISHING ®

www.evernightpublishing.com

BAD TO THE BONE

Copyright© 2018

Sam Crescent

Editor: Karyn White

Cover Artist: Jay Aheer

ISBN: 978-1-77339-669-9

ALL RIGHTS RESERVED

SAM CRESCENT

DEDICATION

I dedicate this to all the MC lovers out there.

SAM CRESCENT

BAD TO THE BONE

Dirty Fuckers MC, 1

Sam Crescent

Copyright © 2015

Prologue

James opened the doors to the old abandoned building. It was large with four floors with plenty of room on the ground floor for them to have a bar, church, kitchen, sitting room, games room, and a couple of other rooms as well. The place needed a lot of work, but with the right vision and plenty of cash, James saw it being a dream for what the MC wanted. They were Dirty Fuckers, and his brother Leonard had decided they should be known as the Dirty Fuckers MC. They were all best friends, and most of them had grown up together in foster care or some of them were runaways.

Each of them had gotten by through working their skills from fighting to fucking. James trusted each of his brothers with his very life. They were not the kind of MC club that dealt guns or drugs, or did illegal shit. They were a bunch of vicious men who'd gotten their name because they dealt in sex and fights. Each of them had worked for Ned Walker at some point, yet none of them had stayed, and that was going back a good five years. They were together forming their own family, united in their loyalty to each other.

"What the fuck is this place?" Drake asked,

coming in behind him.

There were only a couple of brothers who'd followed him to the clubhouse. Some of the brothers were unsure of settling down in one place, but James saw the value in setting down his roots, even if it was strange to him. His brother Leonard, or Pixie as he liked to be called, had also come along with him. James didn't blame him for preferring Pixie. What kind of name was Leonard? His little brother—of a few seconds—had gotten bullied for it through school, but James had always been there to stick up for him. "This place is fucking brilliant." They were the same age, but they were not identical in anyway.

Smiling, James touched the walls.

"How can this place be fucking brilliant? It's falling apart?" Caleb asked, touching the wall.

"Structurally it's sound. There's not a problem with the main building. Everything inside needs a touch of love." James looked around him at the potential. This place was perfection. "Think about it, men. This is going to be our place to put down roots."

The Skulls and Trojans were known for putting down their roots, and it was time for the Dirty Fuckers.

"This is going to drain funds," Drake said.

"We've got more than enough to build this place up. Once we get set up we can open up the bar, have a diner off the main floor, and this back part is the main part of our club. We'll start making money, and we're investing a lot of it as well. We've got what we need to set this place up."

"A diner and bar? What the hell are we saying to the other clubs? Come and fuck with us 'cause we're a bunch of pussies?" Caleb asked.

"No. This is a place for us to party, to fuck, and to stay in the same fucking place." James turned to the men.

"Come on, it's time for us to set up some place. I'm tired of fucking skanks on the road, and beating the shit out of pussies who don't know their dick from their asshole. If other clubs want to come and mess with us, let them. We'd soon show them we're not a club to be messed with."

Everything they did was aboveboard, and no one called them pussies, no one. Even Chaos Bleeds kept away from them. They'd earned their name through hard work, blood, and pain. James would hurt and kill anyone who tried to take on his club.

He turned to Drake, who recently suffered from herpes because he forgot to bag his dick. "You should want to be safe. What I hear that shit fucking hurt," James said.

"So what? We have condoms around?"

"Yeah, we have condoms, and no one can say shit about us. The diner and bar keep us legal, and we can fuck all the pussy that comes through that door." He pointed to the door that they'd just entered.

"I'm in," Pixie said. "I like variety in my pussy."

"You would be," Caleb said. "You never go against your brother."

"I'm living and breathing, which is more than I can say for some people. James looks out for each of us. You need to realize this is a money making pit, and who would turn down free fucking pussy? I'm not. I'm with James 'cause I'm tired of being on the road. I'm tired of having skanky leftovers."

Several seconds passed before anyone else spoke up.

"I've got connections," Drake said, giving in. "We can certainly get this piece of shit up to scratch. I don't know what we'll do for a cook."

"You leave everything up to me. I'll make sure

everything is set up." Taking a deep breath, James looked around the house. This was where they could make their future. The Dirty Fuckers MC was more than ready to take on the town of Greater Falls. He didn't personally know why it was called Greater Falls, but it had a nice ring to it. They were the best MC around as far as he was concerned. Dirty Fuckers MC in Greater Falls. Perfection for him. He couldn't wait to get started.

For the next year the entire club worked on getting the club into something to be proud of. They stripped the interior, and replaced everything that was dead or rotten. James worked side by side with his men, bargaining with electricians, builders, and plumbers. No one fucked over the club. He always got the best deals for his men.

Once the diner was close to being finished he called Teri Davies whom he'd met on the road. He'd fucked her a couple of times, and after he called out her boss, he got her fired. Since then he'd been trying to find the best place for her to work. Teri didn't deserve to be fired, but he'd be a better boss.

He was meeting her at the diner in fifteen minutes. After breaking up a play fight between Pixie and Jerry, James made his way toward the diner just as Teri was pulling into the parking lot.

"What the hell is going on, James?" she asked. "Your cryptic message didn't tell me anything. Do you know how expensive gas is? I can't just come running to you every time you tell me."

"That's why it was cryptic so you decided to fucking come. I'll pay you for gas. You don't need to worry about the cost." He smiled as he held his hand out to the diner. "What do you think?"

She joined him, slugging his arm before turning to the building.

"It's an empty diner, James."

"We own it. The MC owns it, and we're looking for a cook."

Teri paused staring at the building in wonder. "You're shitting me?"

"No."

"I was only a waitress."

"And we tasted all of your food, Teri. You can cook, and you should have owned that fucking diner back in the city. You should own a thousand fucking restaurants. That's how damn good it tastes," he said, meaning every word. "I don't offer shit to shit people. You're good at what you do, the best. I want you cooking for the club, and we'll make sure you're not tempted to walk away."

Tears filled her eyes as she stared at the building. "You got me a diner. This doesn't mean you're going to want to marry me does it?" she asked.

"Fuck no. We're friends, and we can still fuck. I'm not going to own you." He placed his arm across her shoulders and looked up at the diner. "What do you think?"

"I think this is amazing. You finally did it."

"I know."

"This is what Pixie has always wanted," Teri said.

"And I'm giving it to him."

James loved his brother, and when Pixie almost died from a gunfight that they'd not been part of, James had made a promise to himself that he'd find a place for them to settle down.

This was where his brother's dream would start and end.

"Oh my God, you're going to have all the women eating out of the palm of your hand," Teri said.

"I don't want them eating my hand, baby. They're going to be eating my dick."

The Skulls could make a go of it, and he'd just recently heard Chaos Bleeds had settled down, and Trojans MC had always been in one place. It was time for the Dirty Fuckers to have a place, and women were going to be surrounding them like flies around shit.

Chapter One

Five years later

Cora Short glanced across her small apartment to where her friend, Stacey, was wriggling her tits in the mirror. She rolled her eyes at the sight but didn't say anything about how her friend actually looked. Stacey looked hot, but she was trying a little too hard to show off too much flesh.

"What the hell are you doing?" Cora asked. It was a Friday night, and she had the whole of the weekend off. She worked as a secretary at Greater Falls high school. Stacey was the history teacher and a huge flirt, but never crossed the line with any of the kids or flirted with them. Her friend only flirted with men who clearly knew what they could give her. Cora adored her, even if she was a slut most of the time.

"I'm going to that club tonight. I don't give a shit what you say, Cora. I need to get laid, and the only way to do that is to go out and find it." Stacey faced the small mirror and finished doing her makeup.

"I've not got a problem with getting laid. I like having sex."

"You've not had any in forever."

"So, it's not my fault that half the guys here bore me."

"You've just got to take a dick where you can get one."

"I thought you were going after the gym teacher, Bill?" Cora asked, changing the topic of conversation.

"Please, that asshole can't get past his own reflection. He's a waste of space, and I want to experience an actual orgasm tonight."

Cora frowned. "Wait, you're not going to that

MC club are you?"

The Dirty Fuckers MC had spent the past five years gaining a reputation for themselves. Cora had returned to Greater Falls once she failed college, and ditched her cheating fiancé. Besides screwing everything up in her life, she was kind of happy. She'd not been with a guy in three years, but she didn't need a man to be happy. She had sex regularly with random men, but she'd not actually had a steady relationship in a long time. Cora didn't want to have a relationship with just anyone.

The one constant in her life was the vibrator that she owned, and it took care of all of her needs, never cheated, and never told her no. Cora would never admit that she'd named her vibrator Jay. Such a simple easy name to remember, and one she wasn't going to forget anytime soon.

"Yes, I'm going there. I've heard many women come out of there with so many tales, and I want to be taken care of." Stacey started to whine. "I need to have a good night of sex to make myself feel alive.

"I hope you mean not killed. You know these MCs are dangerous."

"Not all MC clubs are dangerous," Stacey said, turning back to face her.

Cora took in the sight of her friend. "You look like you mean business."

"Good. I'm going out to fuck, nothing else."

Rolling her eyes, Cora turned the page of the newspaper she'd been reading.

"You're coming with me," she said.

"Wait? What?"

"You heard, Miss Smarty Pants," Stacey said. "Get up and get dressed. You're going out with me, and we're going to find you some action. I'm not going on my own while you're alone."

"No, that's not happening."

"Er, yeah it is."

"No, it's not, and I'll tell you why. One, I don't feel like going out, and two, I've got a date."

"Jay doesn't count."

She had almost forgotten that Stacey had gotten her drunk, and gotten the truth out of her about naming her vibrator. Cora had threatened extreme bodily harm if Stacey mentioned it to anyone. She would sit on her friend until she screamed for mercy. Cora was bigger than her friend at a size sixteen, while Stacey was a size ten. Cora had never worried about her weight. She ate what she liked, and if men didn't like her curves, they could go and fuck themselves.

"Come on, Cora. It'll be fun, and we can relax, and find a man for you."

Shaking her head, she turned to stare at Stacey, who flopped down on the sofa.

"Fine, I'll have one drink, and then I'm out of there," Cora said.

"Go and get changed. You've got to look hot or the guys don't let you in."

"Are you fucking kidding me?" Cora asked.

"What? It's their club, and what the hell is wrong with dressing up? You're hot, Cora, so put it to good use."

"Sexist pigs," Cora said. What kind of club stopped women from entering or exiting based on the way they were dressed?

Changing into a pair of tight jeans and crop top, she pulled her blonde hair back into a rubber band. When she came out of the bedroom, Stacey looked upset.

"What are you doing?"

"This is the best you're going to get," Cora said, holding her hand up. "I'm not interested in picking up a guy. They're probably all infected with some kind of disease. I told you I wasn't interested in the club. I'm not going to change my mind."

"The hot kind of disease."

Rolling her eyes, Cora grabbed her leather jacket from the back of the couch, and followed Stacey outside. She clicked her car, and when Stacey made to protest, Cora cut her off.

She'd seen many of the Dirty Fuckers around town. They were good looking, but they were also surrounded by women. Cora wasn't interested in following a long list of women who'd fucked the men. She only had a few rules when it came to men, and not being at the mercy of them was one of her rules.

Starting her car, she drove toward the diner, bar, and club. It was one large building that had a large parking lot. The music hit her ears the moment she stepped out of the car. The heavy beat was filled with sex, heat, and promise. She couldn't help but be affected by the noise. Cora had heard plenty of rumors about the club but hadn't believed much of it. Tonight she was going to get the chance to see what all the fuss was about.

The diner was amazing. Cora had eaten there many times, and the chef, Teri was a darling, even if she did belong to the club. Cora liked her a lot, and had tested most of the menu. She was a sucker for some good food.

"Are we eating?" Cora asked, suddenly hungry.

"You've got to be kidding, right? We're going straight to the party. I'm not letting any of those sluts take the best men."

"You do realize you've called a bunch of women sluts for being at this party, right? The same party you're going to."

"I'm not a slut?"

Cora gave her a pointed look.

"I'm not a slut, but I may like acting the part of one."

"You're a slut."

Stacey slapped her playfully on the arm. "Sluts have a lot of fun. Come on, let's go."

Cora followed Stacey up to the door, not seeing the point in arguing with her. There were two men who each had a woman sat on their lap. She recognized their faces but didn't have a clue what they were called. Cora never paid attention to the club before, choosing to ignore them.

"What are you doing here?" the one on the left asked.

"We've come to party," Stacey said, cocking her hip out, pouting her lips.

"What about you?" the one on the right asked Cora.

"I'm here because she wouldn't leave me at home." She crossed her arms over her chest, hoping he tried to piss her off. Cora was more than ready for him. This was the last place she wanted to be, and she was practically begging for them to come at her.

"We only allow party girls inside," left guy said.

"We're only here to party. I want to get laid, too. I'm forever hopeful," Stacey said, trying to purr.

Damn, her friend was really looking for some action tonight. Stacey only tried to purr if she thought it would help. Cora glared at the right guy, wishing he'd say one thing so she could spew filth out of her mouth. Most of the time because she worked in the high school, people assumed she was this sweet little innocent woman who didn't know how to party. The truth was she loved to get down and dirty. The men who tried to date her couldn't handle the kind of freaky shit she loved. They were looking for something normal, and the moment she took over, they ran like fucking cowards. This was why she preferred to keep her relationship with Jay. He didn't complain if she needed to come more than twice a night. No one could keep up with her, and so she hid that side of herself so well, almost no one even knew she existed. Stacey knew, and part of Cora believed this was a ploy to get her dirty side out. Cora hadn't let that side of her out for so long. She'd grown tired of men trying to change her.

Stepping close to the man on her right, she ignored the woman, and focused on him. Her heart was pounding, and her pussy hummed at the simple action of approaching this potentially dangerous man. One of his legs was sticking out, and the other had the woman on it. Stepping so his thigh was between her thighs, she leaned in close so their lips were barely touching, and staring into his eyes, she asked, "What's the matter? Can't you handle a real woman?"

She'd not done anything so crazy in a long time. The thrill of challenging him had her so aroused. Licking her lips, she teased her tongue out, and the way his gaze dropped, Cora had her man. He was thinking of better things to do with that tongue, just like she wanted him to. It had been too damn long since she'd teased a man.

"I think it's time for the club to see what a real woman is supposed to do," he said.

"I think that's a *very* good idea." Cora smiled at him.

"I'm Jerry," right guy said.

"Cora." She shook his hand, using a firm grip. She was a woman, but she wasn't going to come across as a weak one. Cora had stood on her own for a long time.

The door opened, and Stacey walked inside. Keeping her gaze on Jerry for a few seconds longer, Cora finally allowed herself to follow after her friend.

Once the doors closed, Stacey started on her.

"Holy shit, I can't believe I just witnessed that. Wow, you're totally hot. Where has that woman been?"

Keeping her leather jacket, Cora headed for the bar with Stacey following her. "It's nothing. You wanted to get in, and the guy didn't see two party animals. I taught him a lesson not to mess with us, and to give him a bit of mystery." She ordered a soda, not caring about the surprised look on the barman's face. This party animal still had to drive home. "Go, enjoy, taste the new fruits at your mercy." She spoke to Stacey, letting her know that she was more than happy to be left alone.

Stacey didn't need to be told twice. Within seconds she was talking to two men, and Cora leaned against the bar, watching. The club was fucking hot. Men and women were wrapped around each other, and there was no lack of immorality going on. Over in the corner, she saw one guy getting blown by a redhead, holding the woman's head in place as he pumped into her mouth. At the same time he had his fingers inside a woman's pussy, and was sucking her tit. This was the kind of action she'd always loved to be around. There weren't enough clubs like this.

"Does it shock you?" the barman asked, leaning toward her and handing her a soda.

"What?" She took a sip of her soda, finding it cool.

She was burning up. Her whole life she'd been hunting for something like this, and she'd finally found it, in her home town nonetheless. How long had it been going on?

"Everything you're seeing? Some women think

they can handle the open sex, but they always end up having a rude awakening," he said. "The name's Pixie."

"Cora. No, it doesn't surprise me at all." She kept her gaze on the guy who seconds later blew into the woman's mouth.

Licking her dry lips, she remembered she had a soda in her hand.

"This isn't the only room," Pixie said.

"It's not?"

"No, this is for the beginners. For the women who think they can handle it, but really, they can't. The brothers here know how far to go. A woman doesn't want to leave this room, they don't go anywhere."

"It's still free pussy to them," Cora said, finally turning back to the bar, and staring at the handsome man. He had long messy blond hair tied at the back and shocking blue eyes. Pixie was large, muscular, and seriously hot.

"Yes, it's still free pussy. You want to go and explore one of the back rooms?"

"Why would I do that?"

His gaze ran down the front of her body, pausing at her breasts. Her leather jacket had opened, and the shirt she wore along with the bra didn't hide her arousal. Cora didn't make a move to hide her need. She didn't have anything to hide. This was a place to get sex.

"You look like the kind of girl who considers this child's play. I'm never wrong when I see a woman turned on."

Cora stared down the length of his body. "I promised my friend I'd keep an eye on her."

"Who's your friend?"

She nodded in the direction of Stacey, who was dancing between two men.

"She's a little too vanilla for the back room.

She'd not make it past this room where two men at once are considered rather plain," Pixie said.

"Then I guess I'm not going anywhere." Disappointment hit Cora hard. She wanted to see what else the club had available.

"She'll be safe here. I can get Leo and Paul to keep an eye on her," Pixie said.

"Let me go and tell her where I'm headed. I don't want her to worry." Placing her soda on the bar, she made her way toward Stacey.

"Don't you just love bikers?" Stacey said with a dreamy look in her eyes.

"They're fantastic. I've just been offered the tour, one person only. You sure you can handle these two?" Cora asked. "If you want, we can leave."

"Honey, I can handle these two in my sleep. I'm not ready to leave."

Chuckling, she made her way back to the bar. She wasn't going to ruin her friend's time, and she had nothing else to do. "I'm all yours."

"Don't make promises you can't keep."

Pixie shouted someone to tend the bar, and then she was going along with him into hell, or heaven.

****

James stared across the bar as Caleb went to work on Kitty Cat. She was one of them but preferred to be considered a club whore, and one who liked to have some pain thrown into her pleasure. Kitty didn't like any of the other women to know what she was to the club. The other women believed her to be a club whore, but she wasn't. Her circumstances were entirely different. It wasn't his business to tell anyone how to live their life. Kitty Cat was under their protection, and no one fucked with her. Even though she was protected by them, it didn't stop her from wanting to party. Every Friday without fail she was at the club, begging to be let into the back rooms.

Drake took a seat next to him, sipping a can of soda.

"She's a work of art," Drake said as Caleb brought back his leather whip, and slapped it against the flesh of her ass. Kitty Cat's arms were bound above her head, leaving her completely helpless to their pleasure.

Caleb ran his hand down Kitty's stomach, moving to her pussy. She whimpered as he continued to deny her. It was always a push and pull with those two. James loved to watch Caleb in action. He was the most professional out of all of them, and Kitty knew how to take the kind of pain that Caleb administered.

"Pixie's bringing a woman to the back," Drake said.

"He is?"

"Yeah."

"Anyone we know?" James asked, intrigued. It wasn't often his brother brought a woman to come and see the back of the club. This was reserved for the people who could handle just the darker side of pain. Kitty was being whipped again, and James looked around the large room to see another couple of women being played with. Some of the men who weren't part of the club but were loyal were allowed in this part of the club. James had to test them. Across the room was Richard. He was a lawyer, a damn powerful one who loved to get down and dirty but had a reputation to uphold. The club gave him the chance to do what he liked with the women who wanted him. James had tested him out himself, fighting and sparring with the man. He'd put Richard through his paces, and James would gladly patch him into the Dirty Fuckers MC, but Richard only wanted to have a place where he could be himself. The club provided the privacy he required, and the women who knew who to keep their mouths shut.

Right now, Richard was fucking a woman's ass so damn hard that she was begging and pleading for him *not* to stop. Richard didn't have a problem with taking what he wanted in public, or in the club, which was as public as it got. The lawyer couldn't have his exploits being exposed in the public eye.

Turning to the door, James watched a woman with blonde, curly hair enter the room. Her hair was pulled up on top of her head, not too tight, just enough to get it off her face. She wore a tight pair of jeans, a plain shirt, and leather jacket. Pixie's woman had to either be in her late twenties or early thirties. He couldn't be sure. James's dick sure stood to attention.

She paused in the doorway with Pixie stepping right up behind her.

James expected her to run the other way, but she didn't. Her eyes were glazed over as she stared at Kitty. He couldn't look away from her as her tongue peeked out to lick her full bottom lip. Most women ran from this room, but this woman looked like she was desperate for more. Damn, his cock was hard as fucking rock. When Pixie nudged her into the room, she walked, and the sway of her hips was enough to get any man hard.

Pixie urged her to the club, nodding at James.

Well, shit, he wasn't expecting that.

His little brother had brought a woman especially for him. The nod Pixie had just given him was his brother's signal that he'd found a woman to keep him entertained. Wasn't that kind of him? James wasn't going to complain. His body already liked what he was seeing.

"Gentlemen, I'd like you to meet Cora." Pixie eased her down into the booth.

Drake moved down to give them more space.

"Hello," she said. Her voice was sexy as shit.

Yep, James wanted to fuck her. He already wanted to see what her body looked like naked, waiting for him to give her pleasure.

She removed her leather jacket and kept her gaze on Kitty. Caleb had her bent over a spanking bench. The cream was glistening out of her cunt, showing the room that she was completely aroused.

Cora crossed her thighs with her hand between her legs. The simple action had him incredibly aroused. Her tits were rock hard poking against her shirt. She was a curvy woman, a fucking beautiful one. He hoped she didn't have a complex about her weight. James couldn't stand it when women were always complaining about how big or how little they were.

"Stacey's safe?" she asked, looking at Pixie.

"She's more than safe. We're not going to hurt her. Do you want something to drink?" he asked.

"A soda would be great."

James figured she'd go for something stronger.

"Just a soda?" Pixie asked.

"Yes. I'm the driver tonight, and I'm not going to shirk my responsibilities." Her gaze remained on Caleb and Kitty. "Besides, drinking soda doesn't mean you can't have fun."

The couple had stepped things up, and now Caleb was pressing his latex covered cock into Kitty's weeping pussy.

"You ever seen anything like this before?" James asked, curious about her. Drake sat between them, creating a small distance that he wanted to break. There was something enthralling about the sight of her.

Pixie raised his brow at James, waiting.

"No, I've not seen anything like this before. I figured the rumors about this place were false. Greater

Falls isn't usually one for adventure." Cora turned her gaze to him, and James was hit in the gut with the shocking green of her eyes.

"No, it's not."

"You've been here five years?" she asked.

"Give or take. The first couple of years we spent getting this place set up, and the diner. After the first year the diner was all set to open. Teri, our chef, she was more than ready to open. Over the second year, we got the bar up and running, then the club." James explained.

"I only returned a couple of years ago," Cora said.

"What were you doing?"

"A lot of odd jobs in the city and around. I like to move around a lot. My dad passed away suddenly and left me his house. I came back to Greater Falls to take care of business. Before I knew what was happening, I had a job, and I was liking the whole settled down routine. I've not left."

James was intrigued by her. She was the first woman in a long time who'd intrigued him.

"I'll go and get you that drink," Pixie said, leaving.

Following his brother to the secluded bar, James leaned against it, watching her. She hadn't watched him leave or given him any special attention.

"Why did you bring her back here?" he asked.

"She's hot."

"That she is." He couldn't argue with how hot she was.

"She was watching Rex get his dick sucked while he fingered another woman. You should have seen the look in her eyes. I was close to the bar, and just looking at her eyes, I knew I wanted to talk to her. She was fucking into everything that she saw."

"Talk to her, get to know her, or fuck her?"

"I want to fuck her," Pixie said.

"Is that all you want to do with her?"

"I'm not looking to settle down, James. I want to fuck her, that's it."

"You've brought her to me to pick up the pieces," James said.

"You know how a woman gets attached to me. I'm not interested in settling down. I like my pussy to have variety. I'm not looking for forever. Besides, she's your type. She's blonde, beautiful, and smoking hot. I bet she's awesome in between the sheets." Pixie slapped him on the back. "You always have my back."

James looked back toward Cora. She was a beautiful woman, vibrant, and hot. There was something about her that really kicked his gut, and twisted his balls. He wanted to fuck her as much as Pixie did. However, Cora wasn't showing either of them any focus, not even Drake who was sitting beside her. Caleb held her attention while the rest of them were watching her.

"Trade places. You want to use me to break the woman down, I'm going to get to know her first."

"Pussy," Pixie said.

For some reason a lot of the women Pixie fucked had a habit of falling in love with him. James sported a large scar down the side of his face, and women only ever used him for sex. He'd gotten into a particularly nasty fight years ago, leaving him scarred. James had found the bastard who broke the rules in the fighting rink, and fucked up his entire face.

Taking a seat beside Cora, he rested his arm along the back of her chair. She didn't even acknowledge him, simply taking the drink, and having a sip. He wondered if she was putting on an act or if this was really what she was like.

"He knows what he's doing," he said, talking about Caleb now fucking Kitty's ass. The woman really did love to fuck, and in an hour, she'd be begging one of the brothers to fix her need once again. Kitty Cat thrived in the club, and the brothers helped to keep the other bitches off her back. As far as James knew she'd not been with many of the brothers, despite her need. He'd not fucked her, hadn't wanted to. "I can see," she said.

"What brings you to the club?" he asked.

"My friend wanted to get laid, and she dragged me along for the ride. In fact, I am her ride." She rested her can of soda on her lap.

Teasing the hairs at the back of her neck, James finally caught her attention. She turned those startling green eyes toward him, staring right back.

"You've got the same eyes as Pixie," she said.

She didn't mention his scar or anything else.

"I have?"

"Yeah, and no. Looking at them now, your eyes are a brighter blue than his. You brothers?"

"Yes."

"You can tell."

"Oh yeah?" He liked this woman. She was refreshing, and not the usual kind that Pixie brought for him.

"So which one wants to fuck me, and which one is supposed to pick up the pieces?" Cora asked.

James was startled, as were Drake and Pixie.

"What?" he asked.

She gave him a wicked smile. "Honey, I work in a high school, and I've seen all kinds of stuff. I may not teach the kids, but I've seen them lying their asses off to get out of crap. You really need to work on your whispering. You weren't very far away from me, and the music isn't too loud. I could hear perfectly well." She tapped his knee, shocking him further.

Fucking hell, bag this woman, and he'd gladly take her home.

Chapter Two

Cora had caught both men by surprise. *Good.* She didn't like men to misunderstand her, or think she was easily fooled. When she heard them talking, it had taken all of her restraint not to call both men out. Instead, she'd sat back listening to them talk about her. Wow, they really thought she was going to fall for Pixie? Big mistake.

"Oh, by the way, I know the answer to my own question. Pixie wants to fuck me because every woman falls in love with him. Yeah, right," she said, looking toward the guy who'd led her back to the room.

He was actually blushing. It was so cute to see.

"Sorry, boys, I don't play games. No offence, Pixie, but you're a little wet around the ears for me." She finished her drink, and handed it back to James. "I've had better propositions by the jocks in the high school. They also have a little more class about them, and they're teenagers. If you'll excuse me," she said, stepping up and away. She made her way back to the main club. Cora heard them shuffling around, and didn't really give a shit. She didn't even look around to see if they were following. What kind of men did that?

Stacey was in the corner being fucked by one of the men. She looked so happy that Cora didn't want to disturb her. The second guy Stacey had been dancing with was rubbing his cock while he looked at Stacey. He looked ready to blow at any moment.

Way to go, Stacey.

Moving toward him, she tapped his shoulder. "When she's done, tell her I'm outside."

He nodded, and Cora made her way out to where Left and Right were sitting. She took a seat on the steps between them.

"The party too much for you?" Jerry asked.

Rolling her eyes, she glanced at him. "Nah, the party was what I expected. A bunch of teenage dicks in men's bodies. Don't worry. I wasn't expecting a lot anyway. You all lived up to my expectations, but that wasn't very high in the first place."

"Is she fucking serious?" This came from the guy she didn't know the name of.

"I'm very serious," she said. "What's your name?"

"Damon."

"Damon and Jerry, lovely to meet you. Where's the bitches you had on your laps?"

"They got bored, and we'll take care of them inside," Jerry said.

"Wow, this really is a lame assed party." Cora had seen more action in a posh boys' party house, and she should know. She'd been invited to one. Was this what getting older really meant? Going to lame parties, and being hit on only to be passed to another brother for possibly falling in love?

She was thirty years old, and so not ready to call an end to her partying ways. Yet this was the first real party she'd been to in over a year. Most of the time she traveled to the city to allow herself to relax, and spread her wings, and taste the world. In Greater Falls, she had to be respectful.

God, why had she stayed in this town?

You're happy.

In truth, she was happy. Very happy, which was so damn shocking most of the time. She was happy with her job in the high school. It was fun, boring, but never the same. Yeah, the kids could be right pains in the ass, but at least they knew when to back off, and she loved helping them. Everything she did helped all of the kids.

"You think our party is lame?" Jerry asked.

"I've been to better." She stared out across the diner. She saw Teri making her way across the diner toward the club.

"Hey, Cora, I didn't expect to see you here," Teri said, coming close.

"Neither did I. At least Stacey's having some fun."

"Not your scene?"

"It's totally my scene, except for the bunch of teenage boys in men's bodies." She pulled out a piece of gum from her jacket pocket, and placed it in her mouth.

Teri placed her hands on her hips, staring at her. "Wow, you really don't know people, do you?"

"If you're asking if you know me, the answer is no, you don't. It's okay. When the guys are finished with Stacey, I'll take her home." Cora shrugged. She'd be home before midnight.

"I decided to close the diner early," Teri said, looking behind Cora.

"It's okay. The club is full. Boys, you can go on inside, and party. I'll stay out here and steer people away." James spoke up.

"If any of the bitches are sexy as fuck, send them in," Damon said.

Cora glanced behind her to find James, the guy who'd started to organize who was going to fuck her. She was so over bikers.

"The diner closed?" James said, talking to Teri.

"Yep, last customer left twenty minutes ago. It has been a slow night." Teri placed her hand on her hip. Cora recognized that look as she'd worn it many times herself. Teri was looking to get fucked, and fucked well. "Want to come in and party?"

"No, find Jerry or Damon, they'll take care of

you."

There was a few seconds of silence. Then Teri nodded, wished Cora goodnight before making her way into the club.

Letting out a sigh, Cora wasn't surprised even when James sat down beside her.

"Sorry about what happened in there," he said, being the first one to speak between them.

She turned to look at him. He sat on the side where she got a good look at his scar. Cora didn't mind his scar. James was a sexy man. From the moment she walked into the back room she'd clocked him. He commanded a presence even when he didn't do anything. That quality, in her opinion, was rather rare in men. James, he had it, where his brother didn't. "Do you debate fucking women often?" she asked.

"No, Pixie has a problem. A lot of the women who fuck him believe he's in love with them or some shit. He can't handle it, and he hates it when a bitch cries. I'm the one who picks up the pieces."

He held a bottle of beer in his hand, which he offered to her.

"I'm driving, remember?"

"Stacey's staying the night. Leo and Paul are nowhere near done with her."

"Great." She made to stand up, but James placed his hand on her arm.

"Stay."

Cora stared at him before lowering herself back to her seat.

"Thanks."

"I wasn't going to fall in love with Pixie, nor was I going to fuck him."

"He brought you to the back room. It's a big deal with him."

"I didn't argue with him. He's the one who invited me back. Not once did he ask me if it was okay to fuck me. I wasn't going to fuck him, and I had no intention of being with him," Cora said. "I'm here because Stacey wanted to party, not me."

"I'm starting to think this is more your scene."

She turned to him, and he stared right back. "How did you get your scar?"

"Bad fight turned really bad. I more than made up for it."

Cora pursed her lips, but James didn't say another word. "Are you the Prez of this club or just an average member?"

"You know the workings of an MC?"

"Not much. I watch television, and I occasionally party. Ask Stacey, she knows way more than I do."

He chuckled. "I'm the Prez. Pixie's my brother. They're all my brothers. I'd die for them."

"Really?"

"Yes. We've all got each other's backs."

Cora tilted her head to the side. The scar, to her, didn't detract from his looks. If anything, the scar only enhanced his attraction. He made her pussy slick by his look alone. James brought the beer to his lips, and she saw his hands were large, and his fingers looked rough.

Licking her lips, she watched as his gaze moved to her lips.

"What are you thinking?" he asked.

"You're a very handsome man."

He looked shocked. "There's no need to lie," he said.

She laughed. "You're wrong, and I'm not lying. To a girl you may come across as ugly as fuck. To me, you don't." Cora pressed her palm against his face, stroking her thumb over the scar. It wasn't even rough anymore. "How old are you?"

"Forty, you?"

"I'm thirty." She was ten years younger than he was.

He continued to let her touch his cheek, and it took him a couple of minutes before he pushed her hand away.

"You don't want my touch?"

"You're right, a lot of women don't like touching my face anymore." He still held her hand, and was stroking his thumb across her hand. Pulling her hand from his, she touched his face once again.

"Then those women, who were probably girls, didn't deserve to touch you." She went back to stroking his cheek. For a second he pressed his face into her palm before pulling away.

"I'm not a fucking pussy. I don't need the touch of a woman."

He protested way too much.

"It's a shame really," she said, taking the bottle of beer from him and tipping it to her lips.

"What?"

"A woman's touch can be so damn hot if you're with the right woman." She handed him back his beer, and stood. "I'll be back to pick Stacey up in the morning."

"You've just had a drink of beer."

"Don't worry, big boy, I can handle myself." She gave him a wink and walked down to her car. She climbed behind her wheel, smirking. She'd not even taken a drink of beer. Cora had only wanted him to think that she had.

When she finally got home, Cora put her vibrator to use. It was James's face she imagined above her, and his dick she wanted inside her. Maybe one day she'd get her wish.

****

James cut into the sausage, stabbing it into his sunny side yolk. Teri had served him and Pixie first. The rest of his brothers had to wait. Stacey sat between Leo and Paul. Cora's friend had stayed the night, and his two men didn't want to let her go so easily.

From what Leo had told him, she'd called Cora to come to the diner to join her for breakfast. He was still waiting to see if the blonde was as sexy as he remembered from last night. James wondered if he was getting that desperate for a woman, he was starting to make her up in his mind. Not one woman had stroked his scar the way Cora had last night. Surely, that kind of shit was made up in his head.

Cora was the first woman who'd left him rock hard, and he'd spent the whole night thinking about her. No woman had left him like that, not even Teri.

"What's on your mind?" Pixie asked.

"Nothing."

The rest of the guys' food came, delivered by Teri. The brothers only liked food coming from her. All of the brothers had fucked half of the waiting staff. The bitches were known for trying to mess with their food once a brother had a taste of their pussy, and didn't want them for more.

What was it about women always wanting something more than sex? He didn't understand it.

Stacey let out a squeal, and James turned to see the one and only Cora entering the diner. He'd been hoping she was a dog, and he'd only made her beautiful in his drinking. That was not the case. Cora was a stunner, even more so without being slightly drunk. Her blonde curly hair had been left to cascade around her in golden waves. She pulled her sunglasses off, and her green eyes seemed to sparkle as she smiled at her friend. Damn, her body. She wore a summer dress that enhanced her large tits, fuller waist, and rounded hips. This woman was stripper material for those men who liked something to hold on to, and his cock was already rock hard. He wanted inside her sweet little pussy, desperately.

"I'm pleased you made it," Stacey said, leading her toward their table. They'd pulled four tables together for most of the brothers to sit at. Several of the brothers were also back at the club. The club was rarely left unattended.

"You offered to pay for breakfast. I'm never going to turn down free food."

Teri came out of the back room bringing Damon's food.

"Cora, it's great to see you here. It's a bit early for you," Teri said.

"I know. I usually can't wait for your Saturday special. What is it for today?" Cora asked.

James couldn't look away between the two women. Cora captured his attention though, and held it. She took a seat, placing her purse on the floor beside her.

"My mamma's special meatballs," Teri said.

"They sound so good. I'll be back later this afternoon for those meatballs. Your food is to die for." Cora looked in heaven.

Teri chuckled. "I'll promise to make them extra special for you. Now, what can I get you?"

"What's good?"

"My French toast with bacon and fruit butters are amazing," Teri said without looking ashamed to be complimenting her own food.

"I'll have that. I'm ravenous."

Teri disappeared, and James couldn't help but listen in as Stacey and Cora talked. He wanted to know everything about her.

"Two meals out, that's not like you at all. I'm always trying to get you to eat out with me. What about the size of your ass? You always complain about the calories and how you'll have to run," Stacey said.

"My ass is fine, thank you very much. Everywhere you want to eat is boring. I told you, if I'm going to eat out then I'm going to eat good food. You know I run because I enjoy it," Cora said, sticking her tongue out at her friend. "So, how was your night?"

"Awesome, these two men reminded me that I am in fact a woman." Stacey rubbed Leo's and Paul's arms.

"Do you want a try?" Leo asked, looking toward Cora.

"No thanks, boys. I can find my own way of making sure I'm a woman." She gave Leo a wink, before leaving the table to grab her own coffee.

Teri had wanted the diner to be more informal than many of the diners out there, so she set up facilities for people to make their own coffee.

James didn't care about the running of the place. He only cared about the profit he'd make. The diner, Teri's place, made a killing. Teri was a fucking genius in the kitchen. She could take five ingredients and make a mouthwatering meal.

Cora came back to the table with her coffee in her hand.

"I'll go for a run in a couple of hours. I've not got anything else to do today," Cora said.

"Why don't you take Leo and Paul up on their offer?" Stacey asked. "I tested them out for you."

James rolled his eyes, expecting Cora to cave. She didn't.

"No, they're not my scene at all. I told you, Stace, stop trying to set me up with your kind of men. I'm not interested. I can find my own man to fuck." Cora poured some sugar into her coffee, giving it a stir. She looked up, and James caught her gaze. Her smile took his breath away, as it brightened her whole face.

James wanted her underneath him, and he didn't care what it took. He was going to have her pussy.

"I know that face," Pixie said, bringing his attention back to his own table.

"What?" James asked.

"You're planning something."

"The woman you brought to the back room last night," James asked, turning back to find Cora laughing at something Stacey said.

She was such a charming woman. He couldn't look away.

"I want her. I'm going to have her." He staked his claim without caring that his brothers would rib him. Cora was going to be underneath him. The only problem he saw, was she didn't bloody know it yet.

He was going to own every inch of her glorious body, have her begging him for more. James easily could make every single one of her fantasies come true.

Once he did, she'd come back begging him for more.

Throughout the breakfast, he ignored but didn't ignore her. James listened to her talk with Stacey and coo over Teri's food, before she got up to leave. He didn't stay behind. Throwing bills down onto the counter, he said his goodbyes. His brothers knew not to mention where he was going in front of delicate ears. James didn't know what Stacey was about, and he didn't care. Providing she didn't hurt the club in any way, he didn't give a shit. If she wanted to fuck his brothers, he was more than happy to let her keep fucking his brothers. The moment she started fights, caused trouble, pitted one brother against the other, he'd have a problem, and find a way to hurt her. He cared a great deal about his club, and no woman was going to tear them apart, no matter how good her pussy was.

Climbing onto his bike, James followed Cora toward her house. She lived in a small neighborhood where kids still played outside rather than on the latest games. The whole street had a Stepford wife feel to it, but completely modern. Some of the women who came out of the houses were herding their kids out to play, arguing, and cussing.

James spent an hour sitting there, watching her house. He was good at getting what he wanted as he spent most of his time stalking his prey. Cora was his prey, and he'd sit out in front of her house all day if he had to.

She came out of her house, dressed in running gear, and his cock, which had gone flaccid, stood back to attention. Damn, her body was fucking hot. He loved her tits, which were now restrained in a tight bra. Cora ran toward him. Her body was showcased in her running gear, and James had never found something like that to be so damn attractive.

"Is there a problem, biker man?"

"Not at all."

"Why are you watching my house?"

"I've got my reasons."

She smirked, putting the buds in her ears. He didn't hear any music, and in the next moment, she saluted him, before running away.

James allowed her to run. Cora could run, but she wouldn't ever be able to hide. He was far better at finding, and catching, what he wanted.

He pulled his bike into the park that she'd run down to. Climbing off, he chained his bike up, before taking after her.

It didn't take him long before he was running beside her. She didn't stumble, but she did pull the buds out.

"Do you treat all of your women like this?" she asked.

"No."

"I'm special."

"No. You're the one that got away, and you're the one that I want."

She stopped, turning toward him. "What are you doing?" She was taking deep breaths, her nostrils flaring open.

"I want to fuck you like I wanted to last night." He expected some kind of reaction from her. Instead, he got nothing.

Cora rested her hands on her hips. "You want to fuck?"

They were alone, and James closed the distance between them. Banding his arm around her back, he brought her close, pressing his cock against her pussy. Her running shorts were not thick enough to protect her from his touch.

Her gaze went dark as her eyes dilated.

Yeah, she wanted him as much as he wanted her.

He was so fucking hard right now. She rested her hands on his chest, yet didn't push him away.

Banding his arm around her waist, he used his other to cup her ass.

"You know exactly what I want."

"What about what I want?" she asked.

"From the look in your eyes, you want this as much as I do. Don't worry, baby, I don't mind you fighting me. I'll win either way."

She smiled. "I'm not fighting you, biker guy."

"James."

"I'm not fighting you, James. I'm starting to think you're all talk and no action. You've yet to do anything to me." She laughed when he growled at her. "Oh my God, you just growled. Now *that* does sound sexy."

James silenced her when he moved his hand across her hip, cupping her pussy. He pushed the fabric of her shorts up, rubbing through the lips of her pussy.

Her laughter died, and the only sounds that came out of her mouth were those of pleasure. He had her, and she wasn't going to get away. Cora was a mystery to him.

Reaching up, he slid his hand within her shorts, keeping her locked against him. If anyone was to stumble onto them now, they'd only see two people talking closely. They wouldn't know his fingers were inside her tight little pussy.

He stroked his fingers through her slit. She hissed, and he groaned. Her pussy was soaking wet, dripping. James rubbed her slick clit, before sliding down to plunder her tight cunt.

"Now, this can't argue with me."

"I'm wet for you, so what?"

"You want my dick, and, baby, I'd love to give you my dick." He groaned as he thrust two fingers inside her, pressing his thumb against her clit. She'd squeeze his dick so damn good. James couldn't wait to get into her cunt.

She groaned, resting her head against his shoulder. He passed his thumb back and forth, back and forth, over her clit. She was shaking, and James held onto her as she screamed her release against his shoulder. Her teeth sank inside the leather of his jacket, and he kept rubbing even as she shuddered.

He only stopped when she grabbed his hand,

telling him to stop.

Pulling his fingers from her shorts, he brought them up between them. With his gaze on hers, he took his cum slicked fingers into his mouth, and licked them clean.

"Now that is one tasty piece of cunt," he said, trying to shock her.

It didn't happen.

She pressed a kiss to his lips, surprising him more than he had her.

"Thank you so much, I needed that."

Before he got a chance to stop her, she took off. Cora was a fighter, and not a woman easily impressed. He'd have to work a lot harder.

Chapter Three

Cora wasn't surprised to find James resting on his bike outside of her house when she came around the corner. She was fucking exhausted. Cora loved running, but it didn't half make her body ache. He'd taken the edge off of her arousal with his touch. She had surprised him with her response, so points to her.

Pulling her ear buds out, she smiled at him.

"Are you stalking me now?" she asked, walking toward him. He stepped away from his bike, and she couldn't help but look down the front of his pants.

Oh my!

She'd had a lot of men in her time, and seeing him like that, she knew she'd not even come close to being with a man that big. He was huge, rock hard, and thick. He was confined in his pants, and she wondered how good he looked outside of his jeans. She licked her dry lips, unable to look away.

Stop staring at his dick. Look him in the eye, pervert.

Forcing herself to look at him, she wanted to wipe that cocky look right off his face.

"I took care of you. It's only fair."

"Sorry, I'm not looking for a boyfriend." She placed her hand on her hip, smiling at him. Cora wasn't unaware of how much fun she was actually having. He was the first man she'd taken the time to even play with. James hadn't taken off running. He kept coming back for more, and it intrigued her.

"I'm not looking for a girlfriend. I'm looking for a woman who wants a good fuck, and has no limitations in the bedroom. Know of anyone I could use for that?" he asked.

Damn, this man was after her own heart.

"It depends."

"On what?"

"If a guy with a dick that size can put it to good use." She tilted her head to the side, wondering what his comeback would be.

"Let me in, and I'll show you exactly how fucking good it can be between us."

Cora breezed past him. She liked his answers a hell of a lot.

Opening the door, she waited for him to step past the threshold into her home. Cora moaned as he closed the door with her pressed right up against it. James moved fast, which she liked a lot.

He tore the music player out of her hands, placing it on the counter beside her door. This was where she put her keys and mail when she got in the house. James pressed her hands above her head, trapping her between the door, and his body. Core didn't put up a fight.

"This doesn't exactly tell me what you can do," she said.

James ran his hand down her body, touching every inch of her, and yet his touch wasn't enough. Over her clothing, his touch burned, and she so wanted them both to be naked with each other, touching, getting accustomed to their touch.

"What's the matter, baby? Not had a real man?"

"I've not had a real man n—"

He cut her off by slamming his lips on hers.

Cora moaned at the force of his kiss. He nipped at her bottom lip, plundering her mouth with his tongue. She met him halfway, kissing him back with as much fever as he was kissing her.

James cut off from her lips, moving down to her neck. He sucked on her neck, flicking his tongue over her pulse. She was so aroused, and she didn't want him to stop, not once.

"You want me to fuck you, baby?"

"Do you even know my name?" she asked, wanting to keep the upper hand.

"Cora, it's not a name I'm not going to forget." He nipped at her collarbone, and she groaned. The grip he had on her wrists tightened.

She loved the bite of pain as he brought her whole body to arousal.

"Fuck, you're begging for some cock, aren't you, Cora?"

"Shut up."

He gripped her face, not roughly but enough so she had no choice but to focus all on him.

"You want my cock. Don't lie."

James released her hands, and Cora didn't wait for permission. She gripped his cock, stroking him. He was better than she thought he was going to be.

"I want this inside me. What do I have to do to move this along?"

"Bitch," he said, biting out the word at the same time he gripped her shorts, and began to jerk them down her body.

She almost fell over in a heap on the floor. Giggling, Cora did her best to assist him, but it was damn hard.

James took them both to the floor, wrestling out of their clothes. The moment Cora was free, she quickly crawled away from him, ending up in the sitting room. He followed her, and Cora stood to match his stance.

The curtain was open, but no one could see in on them. Cora wouldn't have cared who could see anything. This was her own home, and no one was going to tell her what to do in her own home.

He stepped through into the room, completely

naked. The length of his dick, pointed at her. He really was amazing and long.

"No sex without a condom. I'm not on the pill." She placed her hand on her hip, cocking it to the side.

"Baby, you better get on the pill. I've got a feeling I'm going to need to fuck you regularly to get you out of my system."

"Do you really think you'll get me out of your system?" She couldn't help but taunt him.

This had to be the best way she'd spent a Saturday lunchtime. After her run she'd intended to clean her house, but it didn't really need it.

He held a foil packet between his fingers. "I've come prepared, and no other woman has kept my interest."

Cora wasn't insulted. No man had kept her interest either.

"Were you really that sure?" she asked, glancing at the foil packet.

"Are you offended?"

"No."

"I've always got a condom. You never know when you might need one."

"Boy Scout?"

"No. Prepared. How are we going to do this?" he asked.

James was used to being in charge. His body was covered in ink, and Cora couldn't help but admire his physique. He'd kept in shape entering forty. There was no ounce of fat on his body. He was rock hard, solid, and well worked out.

Moving toward him, she took the condom from his fingers. Without waiting for him to respond, she pushed him down so he fell onto the sofa.

Sinking down to her knees between his legs, she

stared up at him.

"You gonna suck my cock, baby?" he asked, sinking his fingers into her hair.

"That I am. Close your eyes and think of England."

"No. I like to watch."

Gripping his cock, she flicked the tip, and watched him moan. He didn't close his eyes, or look away. His gaze was locked right on hers. Loving his gaze on her, and being a little exhibitionist herself, she went to work, licking, sucking, and putting on a show of lavishing his cock with attention.

Glancing up at him, she saw his eyes were still locked on her. His jaw was constantly clenching as he watched her. Sinking down onto his shaft, she took him as deep as she could without gagging. He released a hiss, and his fingers tightened in her hair.

Working her hand over his saliva covered length, she removed her mouth, and flicked the tip taking all of his pre-cum.

"You're a little slut, aren't you?"

She shook her head. "Not a slut. Just a woman who loves a lot of sex. It doesn't make me a slut."

"Some men would call that a slut."

"Then that man doesn't get my pussy. I don't do labels, and anyone who does, doesn't get me." She'd been with a man who liked to call her a whore and a slut, degrade her for the fact she loved sex. Cora wasn't interested in being degraded. It was the twenty-first century, and yet men still wanted fucking virgins. It was ridiculous. This was one of the points she hated between a man and woman. A man who liked sex could fuck whoever he wanted, and he was a giant stud, something good, and men cheered for themselves. When a woman was exactly the same, loving sex, she was a slut or whore. No, not in her book.

Working his length, she stared into his eyes. "What's it going to be, James?"

"I never had a thing for a slut. I can handle a woman who likes fucking."

She took the condom, tearing into the foil. Retrieving the latex, she nipped the tip, rolling the condom down his length. Cora loved sex, and she believed in her sex being safe. There was no way she was going to risk her health even for an orgasm.

"Fuck, you even make putting a condom on sexy."

"I'm pleased I can arouse you, oh good master," she teased.

Getting to her feet, she straddled his waist, pressing his latex covered cock against her clit. She bit her lip, moaning as his shaft bumped her clit. Cora started to work her hips so that she was caressing her own pussy with his dick. She teased them both with the lightest of touches.

James kept cursing, gripping her ass, and squeezing the flesh.

She pressed her tits to his face, sinking her fingers into his hair as she did.

"You've walked right out of my dreams," he said.

"Be careful with all of the sweet talk, I might start to worry that you actually care."

"If anyone can get me to care, it's you." He began to thrust up to her, bumping her clit with each thrust. She groaned, closing her eyes as she enjoyed the feel of his touch on her body.

"Don't you care about anyone?" she asked, a tiny bit curious about this biker. She didn't think of him as rough. He was intense, yes, intense. Cora wasn't afraid of him though.

"I care about my club."

"Your brothers?"

"All of them. They're my club, baby."

****

This woman was a wet dream come true. James sucked one of Cora's nipples into his mouth, biting down on the bud, even as she used his cock to tease her clit.

"Are we going to start talking about our feelings?" he asked.

"No. I wanted you to be comfortable. You're in my place, with your cock nearly in my pussy. I'm not asking you for anything else. I only want your cock."

"I'm not scared or uncomfortable. Some men would be terrified to have a woman like you in their arms, but not me."

"I've had quite a few men who haven't been able to handle me, and it makes me curious. Why is it that you can handle me?" she asked.

"I know exactly what you need." Moving his hands to her hips, he gripped her flesh, and pulled her up so that only his cock was poised at her entrance. Staring into her eyes, James brought her down, slamming up inside her. He held her so that she couldn't get away from him. Cora was at his mercy as much as he was at hers.

She cried out, arching her back so that her tits were on glorious display. Her pussy was tight, squeezing him to fuck. James knew she'd be lovely and tight, and she was. Fucking perfection. He gripped her ass, squeezing the plump flesh as he leaned forward to bite one of her nipples.

Cora cried out, resting her hands on his shoulders. Her nails sank into his flesh. He loved the bite of pain from her touch.

Lifting her up, he stared between them, watching

his slick cock reappear. The condom was an eyesore, but kids would be even fucking worse. He didn't want kids, was never going to have them. Condoms were a blessing, and so was the pill.

When she got on the pill, he'd fuck her without the condom between them. Until then, he was going to need to buy a hell of a lot more condoms. This woman was smoking hot.

"You ever been fucked in the ass?" he asked, driving up inside her. She ground herself on him, taking him deeper inside her cunt.

"Yes."

He was surprised. Usually a lot of women were not that adventurous. Reaching around, he slid his fingers over the puckered hole of her anus. She didn't tense up. Her eyes closed, and she moaned.

"It has been some time since I've had a dick in my ass." She licked her plump lips, and he couldn't resist taking a kiss.

Moving his fingers down, he slicked his fingers in her cream before taking them back to slide across her anus, driving her wild with his touch.

"You be a good girl, and then I'll fuck you in the ass. I'll let you remember how good it is to have a nice big cock sliding in and out of you."

James had hit the jackpot. Pixie didn't have a clue what angel had slipped through his fingers.

The name Angel reminded him of Lash's woman, and put a dampener on his mood. She was too damn sweet to even be thought of in a moment like this. He wasn't like the other MCs that he knew. He was *never* going to get embroiled in their shit.

She lifted up on his cock only to slam back down in the next instance. He teased her asshole, pressing a little against her puckered hole. James didn't go inside her, even though he wanted to know how far he could push Cora. She was one hot woman. Her body was a piece of art.

If his brothers could see him now, they'd be queuing up for a chance to be with her. She was so fucking hot, and gorgeous.

Cora looked between them, and he followed her gaze to watch his cock disappear and reappear within her pussy. The sight was so fucking good that he'd come in seconds. He didn't want this to end. James wanted to leave his mark on Cora's skin so she wouldn't forget about him easily.

"You like my dick in your pussy?" he asked.

Her moan was all he got.

Watching her tits bounce and her fuck him wasn't how he wanted to go.

Gripping her hips, he tossed her off his dick, forcing her to land on the sofa beside him. He'd taken her completely by surprise, yet she didn't protest. Slamming his dick back inside her, he grunted out as her tight pussy swallowed him down. James had found fucking heaven. There was no question about it. Cora's pussy was heaven.

"I didn't have you as a missionary man," she said.

If he was honest with himself, he hated the missionary position. He much preferred to fuck a woman without looking at her. The moment he started to fuck them while looking into their eyes, they got all weird and shit around him.

Holding her hands above her head, he watched her giggle.

"Oh, you're going to hold me down, James?" she asked.

The twinkle in her eye had him laughing. She really wasn't like any woman he'd ever been with.

He pulled out of her pussy only to slam back inside her. Over and over, he slammed inside her going as deep as the position would allow.

She moaned, arching up against him, even fighting his hold on her.

James held her down with ease, taking what he wanted, not caring if he hurt her just a little bit. A tiny bit of pain could go a long way.

You want her to remember you.

He didn't even want to think about why he wanted that to happen. It didn't make any sense to him whatsoever. He wasn't the kind of man who wanted a woman to remember him. The last thing he wanted was to get close to a woman.

None of those women though, had been anything like Cora. None of them ever called him out on shit.

Last night when she'd pretty much pissed on him and Pixie, he'd been so fucking turned on. He didn't really have much choice in following her. Pixie had lost interest in her. The moment he had to work at pussy, he lost interest. James hadn't lost interest. He wanted her, and now that he was having her, it didn't feel like he was ever going to want to walk away.

Fuck, he was not going to turn into some kind of pussy, chasing after a pussy that really wasn't his own.

"Please, James, I need to come," she said, moaning.

Pushing her hands above her head, he caressed her pussy with his free hand, while still driving inside her.

Each time he flicked her clit, she shuddered against him, whimpering. He was so close to coming himself. Her pussy started to pulse, squeezing him in little flutters as he rode her hard, forcing her to take every inch of his dick.

She came over his cock, and James followed her, filling the condom with his cum. They both cried out their releases, and the sound echoed off the walls. The scent of sex was heavy in the air as he collapsed over her. He'd fucked a lot of women in his time, and not one of them had left him feeling like this.

"I needed that," she said, panting.

"I've wanted that since you walked out on me last night." He still held her captive to the sofa. James released her long enough to move off the sofa. He landed on his ass. All feeling had gone from his body. Not once had he had an orgasm that left him like that.

"What's the matter?" she asked, chuckling.

"Baby, you fucking ruined me."

Her chuckles deepened, and something changed in James. He didn't like it, not at all.

"You got a bathroom somewhere?"

"Yeah, down the corridor. Knock yourself out."

She closed her eyes, resting her palm against her head. He checked out her wrists to see they would bruise.

Leaving her alone, he went to the bathroom to take care of the condom. He removed the latex, throwing it in the trash can. Washing his face, and then his dick, he dried up on a towel, taking it out with him. When he returned to the sitting room, he saw it was empty. Their clothes had been dumped on the chair opposite the sofa.

He listened, and followed the sound of her movements.

She was filling a kettle when he entered.

"I'm making a drink," she said but didn't make a move to offer him one.

"Can I have one?"

Cora raised a brow. "You want to stay to have a drink? Isn't that against some biker guy's code of sex?"

"I don't live by a code. Just what I like to do."

"Then you love to fuck a woman and stick around?"

"No." He placed a towel down on the seat, and sat. James stared down the length of her body, loving how confident she was in being naked. It was refreshing the fact she didn't feel the need to cover up. Her tits were large, with a nice hang on them. James particularly liked her large nipples. They were a thing of beauty. She had a nice rounded stomach and thick hips.

"Do you like what you see?" she asked.

"Hell yeah."

"Don't worry, hotshot. I'm not going to start thinking you're wanting forever." She turned away to grab a couple of cups out of the cupboard above her.

"Why not?"

"I'm not the settling down kind of woman. I don't think I can give up my own space for anyone."

"Have you ever tried a relationship?"

"Yeah, in high school, and I've had a couple of boyfriends out of it. I've also seen how a lot of relationships pan out. Stacey, the woman you met last night, and were having breakfast with this morning," she said, to which he nodded. "She's been married before. It was horrible. The guy was a total asshole, controlling, and wouldn't let her go and do anything. Anyway, he was screwing three different women, gave her an STI, and she walked away."

"Wow, fuck, is she clean now?"

"Of course," Cora said, laughing. "Stacey's a wonderful woman. She's not going to be the settling down kind either. After that asshole did a number on her, she believes sex is the only way. There was a guy at the school who teaches gym who might have had a chance. I don't know what happened, but he's the reason we ended up at your club. Anyway, I'm just not interested in relationships."

"Your friend was using my club to get over a guy?"

"Are you offended?" she asked.

"No. Leo and Paul can handle her. They can handle any chick who wants a good dicking."

She chuckled. "Be warned. Stacey's a handful. It's why it didn't work with her husband. She's a keeper, but she doesn't like to be kept." Cora finished making the tea, and handed him a cup.

"So you don't do relationships?" he asked.

"No. I've tried, and for some strange reason the guys always wanted to change me. I'm not interested in changing. I don't think there's anything wrong with me."

"Nothing is wrong with you, baby."

"Good, and let them guys know they can't change Stacey either."

"I'll let my boys know."

"You do that."

He took a sip of the drink, watching her. "So, what do you do?" he asked.

"I'm a secretary. I work at the Greater Falls High school."

"What would they think of you fucking a biker?"

"What I do on my free time is my own business. Sharon, the principal, is a great woman. She wouldn't fire me for anything like that. All she'd ask is not to bring it to the school grounds." Cora shrugged. "I've no intention of fucking in front of a bunch of kids."

James smiled. They'd give them plenty of ideas, and he sure hoped he'd get a chance to play with Cora again real soon.

Chapter Four

Cora walked back into the diner later that afternoon with James right behind her. She didn't go to his table, nor did she pay attention to Stacey's pointed looks. Her friend was sitting at the biker table once again. Leo and Paul were really close to the woman. The diner was filled with bikers, and Cora stopped when she saw Sharon at a table, alone.

Placing her bag beside Stacey, she held a finger up for a minute. Her friend must have already spoken to Sharon because Stacey didn't pout or complain about being left out.

"Hey, Sharon, you're having a good weekend?" Cora asked, approaching the table.

"I'm not alone. I'm just waiting for Thomas to get back from the toilet." Thomas was the local builder and Sharon's husband. There had been some rumors a couple of months back that Thomas was fucking around with another woman, but nothing came of it. Cora couldn't understand why Thomas would do that. Sharon was a beautiful woman, and he was lucky to have her in his life. "You can sit for a few seconds if you'd like," Sharon said.

Her boss didn't look all that happy.

"I'm not breaking any protocol with having dinner with them, am I?" Cora asked, concerned. Sharon was one of the reasons she loved her job. The woman in front of her was an amazing, kind person. She wouldn't hurt anyone, and yet here she was looking so sad.

"What? Oh, no. I've got nothing against the MC. I can't say their name."

Cora smiled. Dirty Fuckers MC wasn't something you said aloud, at least not in front of tender ears. There were a couple of kids in the diner, but the club's leather jackets simply read "DFMC".

She'd have to ask James about that.

"What's wrong?"

"Oh, nothing. Nothing is wrong. Thomas is on his way back."

Cora stood and watched as Thomas made his way back to the table. He was a sexy bad boy, covered in ink, but he didn't once look toward the club whores who were eating with the MC. Thomas could have any woman he wanted, and he'd been with Sharon for as long as Cora cold remember. When she came back to Greater Falls she'd heard many rumors about the couple, but Cora hated listening to rumors. Most of the time it was all lies and gossip.

There was something going on with the couple, but Cora wasn't going to get mixed up with it.

She gave Sharon a wave, then acknowledged Thomas before making her way toward her table. Stacey lifted her bag out of the way.

"What's going on over there?" Cora asked.

"I don't know. Thomas brought her in a couple of minutes ago. He led the way, holding her hand. She didn't look like a principal when she entered."

"I wonder if the rumors are true?"

"About him fucking that blonde bimbo?" Stacey asked.

Glaring at her friend, she pointed at her hair. "I'm not a bimbo."

"No, but you quit college. What does that say about your species?" Stacey asked.

It was a long running joke between them, and Cora brushed off her teasing. Stacey didn't label anyone.

"I don't know if it's true. If it is, I feel sorry for her. Sharon's a sweetheart. She wouldn't even try to fight or compete with the slut."

There was the label. Cora smirked. Sex did wonders for Stacey's vocabulary.

"I hope it's not that. She doesn't deserve to have her heart broken," Cora said, taking a sip of Stacey's coffee.

"Who does deserve to have their heart broken? I hope it's all lies and it's wrong. Thomas and Sharon are sweet together, have always been."

"I'm going to grab my own coffee," Cora said.

She moved toward the coffee stand, making her own coffee. The diners were allowed to make their own coffee, or get one delivered with their order. Cora loved her coffee a certain way, and she didn't trust anyone else to make it for her.

"You could have sat at my table," James said, coming up behind her.

He placed his hands on the counter on either side of her, trapping her in. He was so much bigger than she was.

Cora glanced over her shoulder and shook her head. "Why would I do that?"

"We just spent the whole of the afternoon fucking."

"So?"

"I figured I'd buy you dinner."

She laughed, swirling a plastic spoon in her coffee. Throwing it in the trash, she turned toward him. "I don't need a babysitter. I never have. I can pay for my own food."

"A guy offering to buy you food is not babysitting you."

"We had some fun. It's okay, James. I'm not expecting anything." She tapped his chest, expecting it to be over. He surprised her by capturing her hand, stalling her.

"I want another day."

"What's going on?" she asked.

"The afternoon with you wasn't enough. I want to fuck you regularly."

She glanced over his shoulder to see Pixie watching them.

"I'm not interested in whatever shit you're trying to pull."

"I'm not pulling any shit. This is for real. It's me here, on the line in front of my brothers."

Cora had enjoyed the afternoon with him. She didn't have to play the good girl to be with him. He knew exactly what she was offering. The whole experience was rather refreshing.

"Okay. I'm not interested in talking with your club about what we suddenly are. I'm going to eat with Stacey, and we'll go back to my place."

"You don't want to come to the club?"

"There'll be time for that, big boy. I've got to keep my wits about me." She gave him a wink before making her way back toward their table.

"What's going on?" Stacey asked.

Her friend had been staring back at her, waiting. "Not a lot."

"Please, he's giving you fuck me eyes."

Rolling her own eyes, Cora smiled. "We had sex."

Leo and Paul turned, giving her their attention. She ignored them. It didn't matter to her that they were listening.

"You fucked James? The prez of the MC?"

"It's not a big deal—well, his dick was a big deal. I wasn't disappointed, and it just proved to me that waiting can make things just as amazing." She took a sip of her coffee, picking up the menu.

Doing something with her hands stopped her from constantly looking toward the man who'd taken her to new heights of pleasure a few hours ago.

"We hit the jackpot," Stacey said.

Leo and Paul were chuckling to themselves.

"Is anything going on between you three?" Cora asked but low enough so only Stacey heard.

"Nah, we're enjoying each other's company. I don't want to settle down with another man. I've been there, done that, and I'm so not interested in wearing the badge again." Stacey wrinkled her nose. "So not interested in crap like that."

Cora laughed. "I'm not asking if marriage is on the cards."

"Nothing is on the cards other than good sex. I'm not going to do it again, Cora. I'm not going to allow myself to get lost in promises none of them can keep." Stacey sounded sad but determined.

"It's not always like that."

"I don't care. I've been burned once before. I'm not going to be burned again." Stacey looked past Cora's shoulder.

Looking in the same direction Cora saw Teri heading her way.

"Let me guess, the meatballs?" Teri asked.

"You know me so well." She offered the other woman her best charming smile. When it came to her food, Cora was a suck up to the core.

"I'll make sure you get plenty for you to enjoy."

"If I loved women, I'd be asking you to marry me," Cora said.

Teri laughed. "I'd certainly be taking you up on that offer."

When Cora turned back toward the table, she saw James was looking at her. He wasn't paying any attention to anyone else but her.

"He's got a thing about you," Stacey said.

"Nah, we're just going to have a good time. It doesn't mean anything."

Stacey let it go, and Cora was thankful. She didn't want to keep answering questions about her love life. Cora didn't have a love life. She had a sex life, which she didn't talk about. James was the first man she'd fucked at her home. She usually met men in clubs, and went back to their place. Cora wasn't looking for long term. It didn't mean anything. It didn't have to mean anything, and Cora wasn't about to start thinking flowers or anything like that.

She refused to be tied to a man in any way. Stacey didn't need to know the entire details. It wasn't like Cora was going to ask for the sordid details of her with the two men.

The rest of the meal went by without event. Teri made the most mouthwatering meatballs she'd ever put in her mouth, and the pasta was to die for. Cora loved spicy, adventurous food, but every now and then, there was nothing wrong with simple.

After lunch, she said her goodbyes to the club, climbing into her car. She'd come separately, and James had ridden on his bike.

Cora didn't give him a look as she drove back to her home. She wasn't surprised as he pulled in right behind her, blocking her car in. James clearly wasn't ready for it to be over between them.

Smiling, she climbed out of her car. She was already soaking wet, and looking forward to the rest of the afternoon of fucking him. They'd only just gotten started that afternoon. If he hadn't wanted to have another go with her, she was fine with that. Cora had never been the kind of woman who'd cry over a man.

Without looking behind her, she opened her door.

James took hold of the door before she could close it. She didn't wait around for him. Kicking off her shoes, she made her way up to her bedroom.

If they were going to talk then they were going to fuck while they did it. She was in desperate need for his cock.

On the way up the steps, she started to unbutton her dress. She loved wearing feminine dresses with the soft fabric against her body.

Dropping the dress to the floor, she stepped out of it, going to her bra. His steps followed her upstairs, and she opened her bedroom door, bending down at the bed to remove her thong.

Crawling on the bed, she heard him hiss but didn't stop until she sat with her pillows behind her.

"I thought we were going to talk?"

"We are. I've found bedroom negotiations are always best if they're in actual bed," she said. "That way, we can fuck out our frustrations when we lose."

He opened his belt, and Cora watched the show. James had removed his jacket, revealing those thick arms that had held her down underneath him. There really was something damn arousing about having a man who could hold her down. She'd not always fucked men with thick muscles, but James was changing her opinion rapidly.

"I don't have any condoms," he said.

Leaning across the bed, she opened her drawer, pulling out several foil wrapped packets. "I've got some myself. I'm always prepared."

He chuckled and finished getting undressed, giving her a little show as he did.

James crawled onto the bed, lying beside her. He touched her hip. "So what's going to happen?" he asked.

"This has to be the strangest conversation ever,"

she said, laughing.

He ran his hand up her body, cupping her breast. She licked her lips, and gasped when he pinched the tip. His touch was awakening the woman within that she really thought had gone to sleep for good once she settled into Greater Falls. She'd gone to the city to play as she'd not wanted a reputation in the place she worked. Small towns didn't like having a free thinking, sex-crazy woman at their school. She wasn't sex crazy, not really. Cora just knew what she liked, and didn't apologize for it.

"You're a fiery woman, and I fucking love it. We're fucking, and spending time together. I like you, Cora."

"You don't even know me," she said, biting her lip.

"I don't need to know you completely to know that I like spending time with you. You're my kind of woman, and you're not expecting any kind of shit from me."

"I like my job. I don't want you to start ordering me around, telling me what I can and can't do. We'll never get along if you do."

"I don't want you telling me to change the club."

"I'm not interested in changing your club or who you are." She reached out, taking hold of his cock.

"So we're fucking, and spending some time together?" he asked.

"I guess that's what we are doing. No expectations, no promises, no nothing."

"Woman, you've got yourself a deal."
****

Several hours later James walked back into his clubhouse pretty damn happy with himself. He'd only just left Cora, and he was more than sated. Entering the clubhouse, he saw Leo and Paul were sitting at the bar nursing a drink. There was no sign of Stacey, or Pixie. He wondered what had sent them off looking gloomy. Both men were usually chipper about everything. James knew he certainly was tonight. A day between Cora's thighs was enough to make any man happy.

Walking to the bar, he asked for a drink off Kitty Cat. She wouldn't be visiting the back room for a couple of days. Whenever Caleb got into the mood to spank and work a club whore, he made sure they were left more than satisfied. With Kitty Cat, though, Caleb was trying to make her realize she wanted him. Something was going on between them two, and James was making sure neither of them got hurt.

When Kitty Cat leaned over the bar, he saw the welts from the crop across the back of her thighs.

"Thanks, baby," he said, taking the beer from her grip.

"You're welcome, Prez." She gave him a wink before moving down to serve some of the customers. Saturday night was always busy, and they opened part of the club for the town folk. From the look of some of the men, they were in fucking heaven.

This was what he loved about settling down. His vision when he'd seen this place, rundown and in need of some loving, had been right on the money. He'd seen the potential straight away. James had been right, and the club was in profit in every business, which was damn fine.

"How was your afternoon?" Leo asked.

"I spent it balls deep in the best pussy in town." James saw both men share a look.

"What?"

"Stacey's pretty damn fine."

He paused with the beer against his lips. "Is that

going to be a problem?" He gave a quick thought to Cora. She wouldn't like it if her friend got hurt, or if Leo and Paul started to pursue Stacey, if she didn't want to be pursued. Damn, he hoped this kind of shit didn't get complicated.

"Don't know what you mean?"

"You fucking do. Stacey's left her mark on you." James needed to make sure it didn't cause any problems for him and Cora. He liked her, and wasn't ready to let her go.

"No, she's special, but not unlike any other pussy," Paul said, clearly trying to sound detached. His face was telling another story. If it was just any pussy, a guy didn't look like he was being torn in two.

"Fuck, you like her?"

"So what? She was different, and she could handle the two of us. She's not like every other woman, and she didn't play favorites, or try to see if one of us would fight for her."

Paul and Leo were known for sharing their women. Some women had even tried to get the boys to fight each other for a chance to fuck her. That wasn't something James liked. Fortunately, both men had turned the pussy down before they would fight with each other. Sharing a woman wasn't unheard of around the Dirty Fuckers MC. They had all shared a woman at some point, and none of them cared if someone was watching as they fucked. James wondered if Cora would give a shit if he bent her over the pool table and took what he wanted from her with the guys watching. He wouldn't let them join in unless she wanted them to.

His cock began to swell, and he forced himself to focus on the two ugly fuckers in front of him. They were never going to be the kind of people he wanted to help with his problem. His swelling dick was only ever going to be satisfied by a woman. He needed to focus on his men, not on himself.

"She took your cock, didn't pass out or complain, and you're in love?"

"We're not in love, and she's not interested in anything more. Anyway, you had a good afternoon?" Leo asked, changing the subject.

The two men *were* in love, and they didn't even know it yet.

Rolling his eyes, James took his beer, and left the two men to pout. Two women had entered their club, and now he was at risk of two of his men wanting to settle for one woman. Well, it wasn't his problem. If Stacey was anything like Cora, he understood the two men.

Heading toward the back room, he saw Pixie was sitting there, watching Richard, the lawyer, at work once again. Wow, it had to be a hard case Richard was working on for him to have spent another day at the clubhouse in the same week. Usually Richard liked to have plenty of time between visits, but this was his second time in the same week.

Taking a seat, he saw Drake was also fucking another woman in the corner. James didn't know who the woman was, and wasn't interested in finding out. Part of him wished he was still back at Cora's house, bringing her to orgasm again.

"What's going on?" he asked.

Pixie glanced over at him. "Not a lot. Richard turned up desperate to relieve his stress. Chloe was more than happy for him to work her over. It has been a long time since Richard worked with her."

"Wasn't that because she was worried she was starting to fall in love with him?" James asked.

They were not a place to offer up their women for sex. The women were free to fuck and do whoever they liked. None of the women would ever get hurt at the club. In fact, one woman had been visiting the club, Laura he believed her name was, and she'd taken a guy to the backroom, and the bastard had gone fucking crazy on her, hurting her. He'd locked Laura inside one of the rooms, and they'd heard her screams and cries for help. All of them had banded together, broken the door down, and taken the fucker out. By the time the night was over, Laura had been taken care of, and the guy was never seen or heard from again. They didn't offer their women up for sex. The women who came to the club were free to do whatever they wanted, within reason. What James wouldn't have is his women upset or hurt.

It had been Chloe who came to him worried about her feelings for Richard. She was a sweet little thing and wouldn't ever harm anyone. She got along well with the club, and James liked her. She worked hard at the diner, and was part of the club. The club was more than happy to help her out. If she wanted to, she fucked any of the brothers she could. If she didn't want to, they still offered her protection. They didn't go swapping protection for sexual favors. They were not that kind of club who needed to bribe women for fucks. There was plenty of pussy available for all of them.

"Chloe said she could handle it, and if he needed her, then she was more than happy to help him." Pixie shrugged. "I'm not going to start telling her what she can't do or not."

James looked toward Richard and Chloe, really not liking it, but there was nothing he could do. Richard wasn't a cruel man, and he'd keep Chloe in the picture. They were well suited together, and it had been Chloe who took a step back from Richard, not the other way around. He recalled Richard had been pretty upset when Chloe wouldn't have anything more to do with him. Still,

Richard had backed down, and given Chloe the space she needed.

"What's going on with you and Cora?" Pixie asked.

"Wow, it has been an entire day and you still know her name. I'm surprised."

Pixie rarely remembered anyone's name.

"What can I say, I'm full of surprises," Pixie said.

"We've agreed we're fucking each other." James smiled just thinking about how much fun bedroom talk was with Cora. She'd made it fun and exciting.

"That's a step up, I guess. You going to be sharing that?" Pixie asked.

James gave him a pointed look. He wasn't going to cross any of their boundaries just yet. He'd known the woman twenty-four hours, and he wasn't going to push his luck. Cora wasn't a woman you rushed into anything. She'd be ready in her own good time.

"Bitch will probably try to mold you into some kind of fucking husband," Pixie said.

"Don't." James wasn't in the mood to deal with Pixie's childish behavior. Cora was the first woman to turn Pixie down.

"What? She got under your skin?"

"You got a problem with me fucking her?" James asked, glaring at him.

"I saw her fucking first."

Cora's words about them being teenagers in men's bodies entered his mind. Right at that moment, Cora hadn't been more right. Shaking his head, he stood up, glaring down at him.

"Don't even pull that fucking card with me. She didn't want you. She wanted me, so keep your shit out of my face," James said, leaving the room, and heading out of the clubhouse. Sitting down on the outside of his club, he overlooked the town of Greater Falls. It was a large place, more than suited for the club. They had made a place for themselves here, and not one that he wanted to ruin. Pixie's childish attitude had pissed him off. What gave him the right to go all pissy? He'd seen her first, so fucking what? It was James that Cora wanted, no one else.

"He doesn't mean shit by what he says," Caleb said, coming out of the club to sit with him.

"He's my brother and I love him, but at times he really pisses me off."

"It's unusual for a woman to not be interested in him. I watched Cora today, and she was only interested in you. It hurt him. He'll get over it in time."

"Don't give a fuck." James was used to being passed over for his brother, and he wasn't pissing and moaning about it. He wasn't going to lie. It was a refreshing change to have a woman only looking at him, which Cora was. She didn't show the slightest bit of interest in Pixie.

You did get your dick sucked and fucked today.

Caleb slapped him on the back. "He'll get over it. It's Pixie. There'll be other women for him to go chasing around."

"Whatever." He tipped his beer back, taking a long swallow.

"I'm going in. I'm in the mood for some Kitty Cat."

Rolling his eyes, James stayed outside, thinking about everything that had happened just recently, not just in his club but outside. A couple of months ago he'd been called by The Skulls to let him know that Lash had taken over as club Prez. It amazed him at times why they even bothered getting in touch. He wouldn't touch The Skulls and Chaos Bleeds, or their mess. Sure, the leaders were fine—well, Tiny was all right, but James wasn't about to change who he was for anyone. They were both good clubs, but it wasn't something he was going to ever get involved in. There was too much danger with both clubs.

The Dirty Fuckers MC wasn't for everyone, but it suited all of the men in the club. He took another long drink, looking out over the town. Nothing bad happened here. There was no shit, drugs, gunfights, or mess for them to clean up. Unlike the shit he'd heard going down in Fort Wills and Piston County. What happened there was the clubs' business, not his. They had all been part of the fighting world for as long as James could remember. His club wasn't dealing with any of that shit, not anymore. They could all take care of themselves, and the club, but the fact they didn't have to, was a great relief to him.

Cora.

She was one of the first good things to happen in his life. He'd seen her around town. James had recognized her when Pixie brought her to the backroom. At the time he'd not been able to remember where, but when she'd been talking with Teri, he recognized her. She'd been in the diner regularly, and he'd seen her many times around town. Every time he'd seen her, she'd always caught his eye, but he'd never acted on it. There was enough pussy at the club so that they didn't have to go looking elsewhere. James hadn't taken the time to stop and talk to her. He didn't really know what would have happened if he did. Now, he just sounded like a pussy.

"Thought I'd find you here," Teri said, coming out of the same door that Caleb had moments before.

"And here I thought I was hiding," James said. "Can't a guy get a fucking break?"

She took a seat beside him, snagging his drink. He didn't put up a fight with her. She took several swallows before handing it back to him. "There's no fucking break for the wicked, James. You should know that by now." He nodded in agreement, and Teri took another long swallow of his drink. "It was busy at the diner today."

"Business is booming," he said.

"Cora's really something, isn't she?"

"She is." James stared straight ahead of him.

"James, look at me," Teri said.

He turned toward her, giving her his gaze. "What?"

"I've known Cora a while. We're not friends like she and Stacey are, but we talk. She's not like other women."

"And what would you say she's like?" he asked.

"I think you know. She's not the kind of woman who settles down with one man or is controlled." Teri ran her hands up and down her thighs before she continued talking. "I've never seen her with a guy twice in a row. She's happy to have some fun, which isn't a problem at all. Cora's a free spirit."

"Why are you telling me this?"

"I watched you watch her. I care about you, James. You're a great fuck, but I consider you a close friend. I'd hate to see you get hurt."

"Cora's not going to hurt me."

"Not intentionally but she will hurt you if you're after what I think you're after."

James let out a sigh, growing frustrated. "Just tell me what you're trying not to tell me." He was even confused by that statement. Clearly, Teri wanted to say something, but she wasn't being blunt with him. James wasn't in the mood to play twenty questions.

"I believe you're at risk of falling in love with Cora, and she's not capable of loving you back."

He burst out laughing. The idea of him falling in love was completely absurd.

"Laugh, James. I know what I saw. The boys have even been talking about it. She passed Pixie over for you. I watched her as much as I did you. Cora didn't look at Pixie. She was more interested in you. That's never happened before."

James stopped laughing. He licked his lips as her concerns were right on the mark. "I'm not going to fall in love with her. We're sleeping together, that's it."

Teri placed her hand on his knee. "I'm here for you."

"Don't do that, Teri."

"I told you years ago, James. I'm not in love with you. We're friends. You just don't see the difference. We can be friends without love."

James had pulled away from Teri a couple of years ago when he believed she was getting a little too close. Teri had told him numerous times that she wasn't in love with him. Over time, he'd started to believe her. There wasn't really anything else he could do. He couldn't argue with her over her feelings.

"I see the difference."

"If you don't know, you will with Cora."

"Why?"

"Because I've got a feeling there's a chance you could fall in love with her."

James wasn't worried about that. Part of him already had.

Chapter Five

Back at work on Monday and Cora was catching up on everything she'd missed Friday that Sharon had wanted her to do, from writing letters to checking up on exam scores. She never took her work home with her as the paperwork wasn't allowed to leave school premises, and so she always called Monday "catch-up day". Cora didn't need to take her work home. As the principal's secretary, she usually got everything done in school hours. Besides, she didn't want to have any files on the kids in the school at home. Sharon was locked away in her office with another bad boy of the moment, who liked to drink, smoke, and cause fights. He wasn't much of a bad boy. Cora recognized the bad boy type, and Ryan Weston wasn't one of them.

Sure, he brought alcohol into school and smoked cigarettes, but that was as far as the bad boy image went. Not once had he stunk of booze. Ryan may bring everything into the school, but he wasn't drinking it. He sure was smoking, but there you were. Kids smoked, and tried to rebel, and Cora didn't take that shit seriously.

Pushing the latest practice SAT scores into the files, Cora then placed each file into the cabinet. Sharon liked to keep a file on every student at the school. Once the senior year left, they all had the option of retaining their file or they burned it. Everything was loaded up onto the computer network anyway, but Sharon liked to have paper copies just in case. Even though everything was done on the computer, Sharon liked it done a certain way.

Cora wasn't going to complain. When the computers crashed a year back the high school remained operational throughout, and Sharon didn't even break into a sweat. There was a benefit to having a backup file that wasn't located on a computer.

The door to Sharon's office opened. "You're going to need to have a long think about what you're doing with your life, Mr. Weston."

Sharon glanced toward her. "Can you keep any eye on him? I've got a call to make, and it's very important."

Ryan muttered something.

"Sure." Cora didn't have a problem with keeping an eye on the kids. If they tried anything, she'd soon teach them not to with a thirty year old woman who knew how to handle herself.

They were alone a second later. Cora hummed to herself while watching Ryan. His arms were folded over his chest, and his bottom lip stuck out. She couldn't help but laugh, then tried to cover it.

"What ya laughing at?" he asked.

"Nothing at all."

Cora ignored him, staring down at her files. Some of the boys today really thought they were so tough. They'd never had it so easy. Mobile phones, video games, cars, the internet, all the crap wasn't really available to her growing up. She was of the old school of using that historical finding, pencil and paper, the shock. Cora missed those days. She'd seen some of the bad shit that happened with all the modern techs with some of the girls in school.

"You know, they have a whole school network for that shit. Paper is so outdated," Ryan said, pointing at what she was doing.

Raising her brow, she turned her stare toward Ryan. "You think paper is so outdated?"

"Yeah."

"Cool, I'll let the principal know."

"Please, she wouldn't change it."

"I don't know, I think spending the day of wiping your ass on a tablet will make you all realize that paper has its uses."

Sharon was aware of her annoyance when it came to boys like Ryan, or the preppy boys from rich families. Cora didn't mind putting on a smile, being nice and kind, but she wouldn't take shit from teenagers. That was the problem these days. They expected everyone to bow down, and tread carefully. Cora wasn't going to take that kind of shit. She'd been in high school many years ago, and she wasn't going to allow herself to be controlled by that life again. School had long finished for her.

Did the grownups even remember what it was like to be a teenager?

"You can't talk to me like that," he said.

"I just did."

Getting up from her seat, she rounded her desk, and leaned back against it. "Do you really think you're all that threatening?" Cora asked.

Ryan stood up, showing off his six foot frame. James would tower over this boy.

"Sit down, boy," she said, folding her arms, and standing up. Even in heels she didn't match his size.

"I think you're afraid."

"That's where you're wrong," James said, jerking Ryan back by the scruff of his neck. Even Cora was surprised to see James in the high school.

"Dude, get the fuck off me."

James put him in his seat and stood in front of him. "You think it's tough standing over a woman who is shorter than you?" James asked.

Cora was about to interfere when James took the seat next to Ryan. He wasn't threatening in his manner, and she was curious about his presence.

"Let me make one thing clear. That woman

would eat you for breakfast and spit you back out. Don't ever think you're better than a woman, tough guy."

"She couldn't have taken me," Ryan said, folding his arms across his chest.

"No? From where you were standing, she could have taken out your balls. When you were gripping those jewels, she'd have grabbed her stapler, and whacked you around the face. That's just to start off with. Never underestimate a woman, Ryan. You'll hate it," James said. "Besides, it's women you need to respect, and if you think you're going to get a fuck out of a woman you've threatened, you've got another think coming."

"Do you two know each other?" Cora asked.

She'd not seen James at the school.

"I'm a friend of the family. His father was a patched in member, but he took off without a word, leaving his wife with three kids, this guy being one of them," James said. "What do you have to say to Cora?"

"I'm sorry, Cora."

"Apology accepted, and James is wrong. I'd have kept kicking you in the nuts," she said, chuckling. She watched as Ryan went a little pale. He'd learned his lesson.

Ryan actually looked like he was going to break into a smile. He didn't look upset anymore or alone. The way he kept looking at James told her that he respected him at least.

"Good, I've got to talk to your principal, and then your ass is coming back to the club."

"Where's Mom?" Ryan asked.

"She's working at the bank. She called and asked me to come and pick up."

"Let me guess, she asked you to have a talk with me?" Ryan asked, spitting each word out.

Cora went back to work but couldn't help

listening in.

"Yeah, we're going to have a talk. You think 'cause your old man has skipped out, we've passed you over? You're wrong about that. We don't take boys like you in, Ryan. You've got to earn your place, and starting crap in school isn't going to do it."

The door to the principal's office opened.

"Can I have a word with you, James?" Sharon asked.

"Sure. Stay here, and try not to piss off the secretary, Ryan. She'll hurt you."

Ryan didn't move even as the door closed to the principal's office.

"I'm really sorry about that," he said. "I don't know why I did it. I was wrong to have done it."

"Don't worry about it. You're not going to be the first boy who has tried that with me, and I imagine you're not going to be the last."

She went back to humming as she completed the files for each student, putting them into the back as they were practice SAT scores. Every year the high school performed a set of practice questions to try and get the students ready for their actual tests. Once the scores were in, teachers then made sure to study the areas that students were failing in. Cora was putting those practice scores away into their files. Teachers could look at the files at any time, so long as they asked permission from Cora or Sharon.

"You know James?"

"Yes, I know him."

"Do you like him?" Ryan asked.

Turing toward the young boy, she tilted her head to the side. "Yes, I like him."

"You're not asking me to get you a date with him or anything."

Cora burst out laughing. "I don't know who you've been hanging out with, Ryan. I'm not going to try and get a date with your friend. I promise. I'm very happy finding men to date myself. I don't need to use anyone else."

She was saved from any more questions when Sharon and James came out of the room. Cora watched them for a few seconds before going back to work.

"Come on then, tough guy, let's get out of here."

James moved toward her, gripping her elbow. "What's up?" she asked, curious to know why he wanted to talk to her.

"I'll be dropping by to see you tonight."

"Is that right?" she asked, smiling.

"You betta believe it."

Cora wasn't going to complain. She looked forward to having him come over.

Shaking her head, she looked behind her at Ryan. "Take care of him."

Cora really did care about the students who passed through her life. A lot of them didn't have any real clue as to what life was like once they left high school.

"I will."

She watched him leave then moved to stand by Sharon. "What was all that about?"

"Ryan's mother couldn't make it, and James is down as the next available contact." Sharon looked exhausted and it wasn't even lunchtime yet.

"Are you all right?"

"Yeah, I'm fine."

"How are things with Thomas?"

"They're as good as they're ever going to get right now. I don't know. I shouldn't talk about it."

"Sharon," Cora said, gripping her arm. "You do

know you've got friends to talk about, right? I wouldn't dream of spreading gossip around. You can trust me."

Sharon's eyes filled with tears. It was times like this when Cora wondered how Sharon ever got the job as principal. She was such a sweet young woman, caring, delicate, and this job didn't accept much of those things anymore. Women needed to be tough and to show a no-nonsense attitude.

"I appreciate it. I just can't talk about it right now." Sharon tapped her hand, batting away the tears. "Now, I've got to get on about the delivery of three new computers. The money was donated for them, and now I want to see where the blasted things are."

Cora laughed, watching Sharon leave to go back into her office. That was why Sharon got the job. She may be sweet, delicate, and caring, but she didn't take any crap when it came to the care of the kids. Sharon wanted the best for the students, and she bent over backwards to get it.

****

"I wasn't going to hurt that lady," Ryan said.

James glanced across the car toward him. "I know you wouldn't. If you had, I'd have beaten the shit out of you. You're sixteen, Ryan. You know better than to try shit like that. We never hurt a woman like that, or threaten her."

"I know. I'm sorry."

"I mean it, Ryan. The club doesn't accept bullies. You want to be a bully then go and find another town to do that shit in. Last time we talked you told me you wanted to be a patched in member. I don't allow bullies in my club. We're men, we accept our responsibilities, and we work damned hard, do you understand?"

"Yes, sir."

"Good. Cora's off limits. You treat her with

respect."

"Is she your old lady?"

"She's the woman I'm seeing at the moment. I don't believe she'll ever be anyone's old lady."

Lucy, Ryan's mother, had begged him to pick Ryan up, and to keep him for the afternoon. Once he found out what Ryan had been doing, James promised to have a word with the little shit. Ryan's father may have run out of town, but that didn't give him a reason to start acting up. Lucy was doing the best she could, and she was under the club protection.

"What's going on with you?" James asked, pulling up outside of the diner.

"I don't know. I'm angry, I guess."

"Why are you angry? And don't give me shit. I'm not in the mood, Ryan."

"My dad's a coward, and my mom's always so damned busy. I'm tired of it. I'm tired of her expecting him to come home, or waiting for him to call. He just upped and left," Ryan said.

"You've got everything to be angry about, Ryan," James said. "Look, I didn't have a dad to care about. I only had my brother Pixie. I know about the anger. I understand the anger. Being a man isn't about letting that anger control you. It's about controlling that anger, and becoming a better man."

Ryan turned to him with tears in his eyes. "Why did he leave?"

"I don't know, son, I really don't know. You've got to talk to your mother. She's so afraid right now. She's afraid of losing you, and failing you. Lucy's a good woman. She's a strong woman, but she's got the same anger you do. He's your dad, but he's her husband. What is she to do now? She can't move on right now."

"I can't move on. He's always going to be my

dad."

"Exactly. He's always going to be your dad, but what about your mom? What about her happiness? Can she move on? Can she find someone else? At the moment, she can't. She's sitting around waiting for him to come home. Will he ever come home?" James asked.

"Are you looking for him?"

"We're looking for him, but when a brother doesn't want to be found, there's no point in looking for him, Ryan. Your father, he left for a reason. I'm not making excuses for him because I wouldn't dream of leaving my club behind, but we've all got reasons for doing the shit we do." James turned to look at the diner. "Now, we're going to go in there, eat some good food, and talk. No more bullshit from you, Ryan.

"Yes, sir."

James opened the car door and took his regular booth. Teri came over handing out menus. She didn't linger at the table, and with Cora in his life, James was starting to see he'd gotten it completely wrong with Teri. The women cared about him as a friend, like he cared about her. There wasn't any love between them, and there never would be.

He sat for the next three hours talking with Ryan, working shit out with him. The kid was angry, confused, upset, and hurt. James knew all about that, and it was all for good reason. When he was growing up in the foster homes, his anger got him through the worst of the pain. Now, he was helping Ryan get through his.

When Lucy walked into the diner at lunchtime, she looked so damned tired. Several of the brothers had joined him in that time.

He took her arm, and led her to the table in the back. James gave Ryan a look to stay where he was. It had been too long since he'd talked with Lucy, and he wanted to know what was going on. She rarely visited the club, and didn't accept any payouts from him.

"What's going on?" he asked, taking a seat.

The club had voiced their concerns, each bother coming toward him to complain about this shit.

"I'm really sorry, James."

"I don't need to hear you say sorry. What the fuck is going on?"

"I don't know. Ryan's been acting up and different in the past couple of months. Dane not coming home has hit him hard. He really thought Dane would come back."

"It has been over a year."

"I know. I know. I've tried to tell him, but at the same time, what do I say? I don't know what to say. Is Dane coming back?" Lucy pressed a hand to her face. "I can't do anything right now."

"Jerry stopped by your place. Your lawn needs mowing, and you're running out of food. Why haven't you asked for help?" James asked. He reached over putting a hand on her shoulder. She was shaking with her sobs. There was only so much the club could do. Unless they were asked for help, he didn't like the club to invade people's lives, even if that person was an old lady. They were a big club, and Lucy hadn't been around much. Dane was a fucking asshole for leaving her.

"Dane was part of the club, not me and the kids. I know he loved us in his own way, and with him settling down, and moving us to Greater Falls, it was supposed to be a new start. I just didn't think I could ask you for anything."

"Honey," James said. "You're Dane's old lady. I don't give a fuck if Dane's gone walkabout. He'll turn up, and when he does, he'll get the fucking hiding of a life, believe me. We're your family. You've never turned your back on us. Whenever we needed a place to crash before we came here, you were there, Lucy. Food, shelter, you were always there, and you never once turned a brother away. We wouldn't turn you away now."

"I'm really sorry."

"Ryan needs guidance. He needs the club, and so do you. This weekend, we're coming to clean your place up, mow the lawn." James pulled out several notes. "Here's some cash to tide you over. Cut your hours at the bank. Kids need you more than the bank."

"I can't take this."

"You're taking it or you can insult the club."

"James, I'd never insult the club."

"Then put it in your purse, take Ryan shopping, go home, make a cooked meal before getting your kids. You're always welcome at the club. Don't die inside because Dane has gone."

"I can't move on, not yet."

"I'm not asking you to move on. I'm asking you to live." He patted her on the shoulder, herding her back toward the club. Several brothers took in her red face. Ryan looked embarrassed, and he hugged his mother. James saw them both out, checking over Lucy's car before she drove off. "I'll get Pixie to have a look over the car at the weekend."

"Thank you, James." She hugged him close then climbed behind her wheel.

"I feel for her," Teri said when he walked back in.

"Yeah, I do as well." Dane leaving had upset the whole of the club when he left. He'd turn up eventually.

He joined his brothers getting an update on the latest business ventures he had in place. James wanted to open a business within the center of town. They had the diner, the bar, the club, and the investments they made in the stock markets, but he wanted to continue building Greater Falls, not just for the club, but for the people. The town was going to become their whole family. He wanted to give back to the community, and find a place for families like Lucy.

There were three buildings up for sale, one next to the large mall, the other by the supermarket, and then a small place near the library. None of the locations were ideal, but he didn't know exactly what to do.

"We'll keep looking and thinking. The town already has a gym," James said, leaving the diner at five. He'd kept himself busy so he wouldn't just turn up at her apartment looking like he was desperate.

He climbed into his car and drove toward her house. The sun was setting, and there was a slight chill in the air. When he pulled up outside of her house, he saw she was in the garden, talking over the fence with a man in his late sixties.

James joined her, nodding his head at the neighbor.

"Bill, I'd like you to meet James. James, this is my neighbor and flower expert, Bill. He keeps me on my toes with his advice, and my flowers look amazing."

Leaning over he shook Bill's hand to find he had a strong grip.

"Are you going to be taking care of this petal here?" Bill asked.

"Bill, seriously?" Cora asked, going a little red.

"I certainly will, sir."

"Sir, I like that," Bill said.

James chuckled.

"I've got no problem with you leather types. When you first moved in the neighborhood I told our Maureen, we'd have to leave. Now, I get more worried if someone normal moves in."

Cora laughed. "Please, Bill, you were worried about me living here."

"Not at all. You've lived here before. Anyway, I better go inside. Have a lovely evening, you two."

"Sleep well, Bill," Cora said.

James followed Cora inside. She wore a pair of shorts and a shirt covered in dirt.

"You been getting your hands dirty?"

"I like a bit of gardening. It relaxes me. I was going to go for a run, but I didn't want you to accuse me of running away." She pulled out a pitcher of tea. "Want a drink?" she asked.

"Yeah."

He took a seat at her counter, and watched her. This was what he could get used to, and now he understood exactly what Teri was talking about.

There was a high risk of him falling in love with Cora. A very high risk.

Chapter Six

"Are you going to spend the rest of the day watching me?" Cora asked, handing him the tall glass of tea. She liked it when he looked at her. His attention gave her a thrill, and it turned her on.

"Nah, just a couple of hours, I think or until I get bored."

She chuckled. "Did Ryan get home okay?"

"Yeah. It's sad news."

"I'm not going to pry if it's private." She wasn't interested in gossip, especially if it was all lies. It was the one downside to living in a small town. There was so much gossip that was complete lies.

"Not really private. Long story short, Ryan's the kid of one of the patched in members, Dane. You ever met him?"

Cora took a long swig of her drink, thinking. "Twice, I met him. Once he had to come in and settle some kind of trip money that had gotten lost. The next time was at a parent-teacher night. I don't recall him recently though."

"Well, about a year ago, he went off to the supermarket, and he's not been back since. There's no sign of him anywhere." James sat back, removing his jacket as he did. She licked her lips, imagining him completely naked. "The brothers have searched for him. Admittedly, we've not broken our backs trying to find him. We're from a certain way of life. If we want to go, we go. There was not even a sign that he was going to leave."

"Certain way of life?"

"None of us had any family before the club. We're all from foster homes or ran away from home. Kitty Cat, the woman you saw getting the spanking of her life, and her ass fucked, she was one of the women we grew up with."

His words were only making her hot around the edges. She remembered that scene, and it had been damn hot.

"Dane hasn't come back?"

"No. He's gone, and I don't know if he's coming back. He didn't take his leather cut, so I've got a feeling he's looking for something he'll never find."

"What's that?"

"To wipe away the past." James shrugged. "We've all got a past we're not proud of."

"Is that because of your scar?" Cora asked, pointing her own nose.

"No. That just pissed me off when I got it. I had a damned good face until that fucker."

She chuckled. "You've got a handsome face now." Rounding the counter, she pressed her palm to his cheek, tracing the scar. "It's an old scar."

"It was an old life, not one I'm doing again anytime soon."

Cora licked her dry lips as his hand rested on her hip. The clothing she wore was light, and she felt his touch like a brand through her skin.

"What about you? Are you trying to run away from a past?" he asked.

"No. I'm happy with my past."

"Tell me about it."

Taking a sip of her drink, she closed her eyes, enjoying the feel of his fingers touching her skin. She liked having her body stroked, caressed. What woman didn't?

"I went away to college to study business and the law."

"You're a graduate?"

"No. Not even close. One day I was running to class, scared out of my mind about missing the lecture, and I was about to cross the road when I watched a car run over a woman." Cora hadn't thought about that incident in so long. "I had stopped at the traffic lights because I saw them go green for the cars to go. It was so surreal as it happened. This car came around the corner, going at the normal speed, and this woman, this businesswoman, was so busy, so preoccupied on the phone that she didn't even look up to see what was happening. She stepped out into the middle of the road, talking with a client, and in the next moment, she was underneath the car." Cora stopped for a second, biting her lip. "It went all a bit crazy. I ran over the road, kneeling down, and I tried to talk to her. The guy in the car climbed out. We couldn't move the car. She was under it, and we waited for the emergency services to arrive. I held her hand the entire time. I couldn't do anything but hold her hand. She was crying, and there was blood." Tears filled Cora's eyes as she recalled the horrid scene. "She kept saying that she only needed one more client to make partnership. That call she was on would have finalized her partnership deal at a law firm. She died at the scene."

"What happened then?" James asked.

She turned her gaze back toward him. "I promised myself that it didn't matter who it was, or what I had to do, I'd never risk my life in order to gain something. There was a hell of a lot more to life than studying, rushing to class, losing sleep, losing life itself. I didn't become some drug-taking whore, or anything. I just decided that I was going to college, studying law and business to make my father proud." She smiled. "He was proud of me just for graduating high school. I'm pleased I never went back to college. I've never regretted what I did. I stayed away from Greater Falls, but my dad came and visited me often, a hell of a lot more than if I'd been in college. We grew close and stayed close, and he thought it was good that I was living my life the way I wanted to live it." Cora let out a sigh. "Wow, I never thought I'd tell anyone else that story."

"Who else knows?" he asked.

"Stacey, she knows what happened. The way I see it, the college life isn't for everyone. It didn't suit me. I wish it did, but it didn't. I'm happier now than I've ever been. I do believe you've got to do stuff in life that makes you happy, not everyone else. It's where we all start to make mistakes. We live life by trying to make others happy."

"I agree."

"So, we've given each other a little information about ourselves."

"I'm going to be heading over to Lucy's with some of the guys this weekend. If you'd want to come, you're more than welcome to."

"You're inviting me to another woman's house?"

"We're mowing the lawn and doing some work."

"Lucy Weston? The woman who works at the bank in town?"

"That's her, why?"

"Ah, I know her. She's nice, and she made a peanut butter chocolate pie a couple of months back. I need the recipe, and what better way to get it?" She gave him a smile.

James ran his finger under the edge of her shirt. The moment he touched skin, she wanted to moan. Instead, she took another long drink of her cup.

"Nothing fazes you?"

"A lot of things faze me. I just choose to ignore it," she said.

He pushed back on the stool, making room for her to stand. He began to tug down her shorts. Putting her glass on the counter, she wriggled along with his movements, until she stood before him naked.

She wasn't wearing any underwear underneath her shorts. Opening her thighs, she moaned as he skimmed his fingers up the inside her leg. Biting her lip, she couldn't hold her head up as he touched her.

"You're wet, Cora."

"It's what you do to me."

He lifted her up onto the counter. She hissed at the cool counter against her ass but didn't move away.

James stood, pushing his stool out of the way. He pressed a hard kiss to her lips, and Cora responded. How could she not? It was so damn hot having his lips on hers.

This was what she was enjoying. The time they spent together was so easy. There wasn't anything too challenging, and they didn't argue with each other. It was simple, easy, and calm.

"I'm going to lick your pussy."

"Feel free."

He opened the lips of her pussy, sliding a finger up and down her slit, going around her clit, then gliding down to press inside her. Cora went from watching him, to watching his fingers on her pussy.

When he leaned down and sucked her clit, Cora truly believed she was going to explode from the pleasure. She'd not seen him Sunday, and it was only Monday, yet it had felt like weeks had passed since he'd touched her.

"I love how you taste, and you're always so ripe and ready."

"Please, James, I need to come."

"Are you going to come all over my tongue?"

"Yes, fuck." She hissed as he bit down on her clit.

An explosion of pain ran throughout her body followed by pleasure, numbing that too-sharp thud of pain. She was torn between pushing him away, and drawing him closer, and not letting him stop.

He licked down to her entrance, and penetrated her with his tongue. She lifted off the counter, and fucked herself on his tongue. James gripped her hips, stopping her as he brought his tongue back to her clit.

She cried out as he repeatedly flicked her clit with his tongue. James teased and tormented her, taking her to the peak of pleasure and holding her there, never letting her go over the edge even though it was what they both wanted.

The moment she came, she'd impale herself on his cock.

"Please, James, please."

It didn't matter about the number of pleas she gave, he continued to hold at the edge, teasing her, testing her limits. Cora didn't know how long she'd be able to hold on until finally he showed her mercy. He plundered her into a screaming orgasm that left her shaken, gripping onto the counter for support as she truly felt she was falling.

He continued to lick her clit, prolonging the sweet bliss he'd wrought on her body.

"Please, please, please," she said, sinking her fingers into his hair to stop him.

James eased back, pressing a kiss to her stomach. He looked up at her with his chin glistening from her cream. He didn't make a move to wipe it away, and that only turned her on more.

Cora jumped from the counter, and with his grip on her hips, he spun her around. The sound of his belt clanging together, echoed in the kitchen. He tore into a foil packet, sliding it on his dick, as she opened her legs wide enough for him to fuck her.

He eased the tip of his cock at her entrance, and glancing over her shoulder, she watched him. James was too busy looking at his cock to see her face.

She didn't need to see what he was doing, as she felt everything. He pressed the tip of his cock to her entrance, gripping her hips with both hands. Crying out, Cora slammed down on his dick, and he plowed inside her, fucking hard. He filled her, stretching the walls of her pussy with the width of his cock.

"Fuck, Cora, you're tight."

Holding onto the counter for support, she started to work her hips, and fuck him right back. He didn't let go of her hips even though his touch was bruising. Cora didn't complain. She loved it when he marked her. The dots of his fingers on her hips only served to remind her of the great sex she'd experienced in his hands before they began to fade. Every time she looked in the mirror, she'd see the marks, and know they had some good sex.

Neither of them rushed to the end. James eased inside her, going slow, then slamming in the last few inches until he hit the hilt inside her.

Perspiration dotted their skin, and Cora couldn't think of a better way to spend her evening than fucking James.

****

James wiped the sweat from his brow as he looked across the back yard to see Cora, Stacey, Teri, and Lucy talking. Kitty Cat was there as well, but she wasn't talking. She smiled along with the other women. Cora had linked her arm through Kitty Cat's. It was as if she knew that Kitty Cat wasn't someone who was easily sociable. She'd never gotten along with many of the women who flitted in and out of their lives. Cora wouldn't let that faze her though.

"It's great to be here," Damon said, standing beside him. They were all doing little jobs around the garden. James had mowing duty, which would have been easier with a gas mower. Leo and Paul were cleaning the pool. Damon was cleaning the porch.

Several of the brothers were repairing the outside and inside of the house. The jobs they were all doing were the same jobs James remembered Dane asking him about. Why they hadn't come to fix the place then, he didn't know. With Dane missing, it had all just slipped his mind. Ryan was weeding through the flower patch. The other two kids were playing around, chasing each other with a brush.

Once they were all done, they were going to fire up the grill, and have a few steaks and burgers.

"They look good together," Pixie said, joining them.

"Yeah, they do."

Cora broke away from the group, bouncing up to him with Kitty on her arm. "Guess what?"

"What?" he asked. He couldn't help but smile back at her. She looked so damned happy with herself.

"Lucy has promised to share with me her amazing peanut butter pie recipe. If you play your cards right, we'll be eating some of that very soon." She stepped up to him, planting a little kiss on his lips.

James was aware of his brothers watching him. This was the first time in the history of a club where a woman had been so relaxed around him, talking to him, kissing him.

"I've also decided to adopt Kitty Cat," Cora said.

Stacey moved behind them, placing her arm across Kitty's shoulders.

"Yes, she's our new sister. She's no longer Kitty Cat, though, she's Kitty."

From the look on Kitty's face, she was so damned happy about that. She'd been around the club a long time. He'd not even given it much thought if she wanted to be around all of them.

Leo and Paul were staring at Stacey intently. It was always James's job to make sure his brothers were dealing with shit.

"What's this going to mean for the club?" James asked.

"Oh, we're having a girly night tonight. You're not invited back to my home. Kitty's going to stay with me," Cora said.

Stacey laughed, pointing at his face.

"It's nice to know you're going to miss me." Cora kissed him again, moving across the garden.

"What's going on with you and Cora?" Pixie asked.

"We're having some fun."

"She's right though, you look damned gutted."

"If you knew what Cora was like in bed, you'd know." James threw his shirt over the handle of the lawnmower, and got back to work. He pushed the mower back and forth, watching as Cora got stuck into work. She helped Ryan through the weeding. He was … happy, and he knew it was because of Cora. She had an easy way about her. There was nothing fake or mean about her, unlike some women.

He really did like her.

Someone turned some music on, and it wasn't long before everyone started to dance. Lucy walked out of the house with drinks, and when she passed by, James snagged one. "How are you feeling?" he asked.

"I'm feeling better. This is amazing. I completely forgot what it was like to have you all here. I've missed this. I've missed you."

He took a long drink. "We're here for you."

"I like Cora. She's such a wonderful person. Ryan speaks highly of her."

James glanced toward Ryan. He was dancing around the garden with Stacey and Teri. Leo and Paul were not looking too happy about that.

When a song came on about a woman no longer accepting a man cheating on her, the women stood in a circle, jumping, and miming along to the words. James leaned on his mower and watched Cora. Her eyes were glowing with life, and he recalled the story she'd told him about witnessing the death of a businesswoman. It had affected her in such a fundamental way. If she'd not witnessed it, and she hadn't changed, he doubted they'd have ever been in the same garden, singing to trashy pop songs.

Leo and Paul snagged Stacey around the waist. Cora's friend laughed at the action, but there was nothing there for her. His men were going to get hurt if they thought they could tame that wild cat. She taught history at the school and was a damn good teacher, but she wasn't going to settle with one man, let alone two.

Since Cora and Stacey had visited the club James had done some digging on them. Neither woman had a bad reputation, but they were known for being together without men. Teri got along with both of them well.

Cora danced toward him, pointing her finger in his direction. He usually hated being the focus or the main attention, and some of the club turned to watch them. James stepped away from the lawnmower as Cora moved right up to his body. She wasn't singing. She mimed as she wrapped her arm around his neck, bowing back. He dropped her a little. She didn't once break the flow of the song.

He brought her back up, and Cora turned in his

arms, dancing down his body, going back up, touching him with her hand.

She circled him, and James followed her, catching her hand, and tugging her back. He never danced, and yet Cora had pulled him into the song, warning him about leaving.

Pulling her toward him, they were a breath away, and the song ended. James slammed his lips down on hers, claiming the kiss he'd been dying to do for so long.

The brothers erupted, whistling, and whooping at the kiss.

"I don't dance," he said, pulling away.

"I do, and if you want to get with me, baby, you better learn to kiss me back." She stroked his cheek, and pulled away. "There's going to be a lot of firsts between us." Cora gave him a wink, then walked away.

"You're fucked," Pixie said.

"Jealous?" James asked.

"Fuck, yeah, I'm jealous. You've got an amazing woman right there, and I let her slip through my fingers."

James couldn't argue with his brother there. After they cleared away the mess they fired up the barbeque, grilling up some burgers and steaks. There wasn't enough, so Cora and Ryan left to get some more from the store. They were back in twenty minutes, and in the short time of being around the club, Ryan looked happier.

Nodding him over toward him, James handed him a burger. "How are you feeling now?"

"I'm doing good. I missed this. I didn't think I was ever going to get this again."

"The brothers never left you, Ryan. We're not like that. We just got busy. I promise, it's not going to be like that anymore."

"I believe you." Ryan looked over to the women. James followed his gaze to find Cora and Stacey having handstand competitions. Cora's shirt had rolled up her body, but she was wearing a sports bra. They were all dressed in gardening clothes.

"Get your mind out of the gutter," James said, tapping the back of his head lightly.

"She's hot."

"And she's older."

"Cougar."

James snorted. Cora was all his, and when he shared her, it was only going to be for a chance to blow her mind, no other reason. He wasn't going to spring sharing her with another member yet. She was adventurous, and he wanted to put his stamp on her.

Every time he thought about Cora, he couldn't stop thinking of her as his.

Mine.

Pixie had shown too much jealousy, so he wasn't going to share her with his brother. One day he'd broach the subject with her, but not yet. He didn't want to risk losing what they had with each other.

James loved sharing, getting the opportunity to watch his woman come apart by the touch of another man. It wasn't for everyone, but it was for him.

"I won, Stace, in your face," Cora said, hugging her friend close.

"I demand a rematch."

While they were waiting for the next wave of food, Cora challenged Stacey, Lucy, Teri, and Kitty Cat to see who could stay up the longest.

"Come on, James, show her how it's done," Pixie said.

Cora was becoming loved by the club. They had all come up to him to say how much they adored her.

"You can do handstands, big boy?" she asked.

"I don't know how long for." He went for

modesty. Growing up, James had watched a bunch of girls do it at the foster home where he was staying. When he found himself thinking too much about life, he started to do it. He used to rest against a wall, staying on his hands for minutes at a time. That was years ago. "This is childish."

Cora blew a raspberry. "No, it's not. It's fun. Come on, we were all children at one time, and they have a hell of a lot more fun than we do. Can't beat them, join them."

Rolling his eyes, he walked up toward her. "You asked for it."

Stacey counted to three, and they both went on their hands. Closing his eyes, James focused on keeping his body straight up. He worked out every other day to keep his body in shape.

"Come on, Cora, keep it together," Stacey said.

Opening his eyes, he saw Cora was wobbling. The moment she collapsed, James lowered himself back down. Banding his arm around her waist, he pulled her up against him.

"You've been holding out on me," she said.

"Not really." He kissed her hard, and deep. "Now that is much better than being a kid." James nipped her lips playfully.

Chapter Seven

"You've known James and the club all of your life?" Cora asked, placing the large tray filled with dips onto the table. Teri, Stacey, and Kitty Cat were back at her place. Lucy couldn't get a babysitter, and none of the other women wanted to come.

"Well, not all of it. We ended up in foster care together. I was the youngest. I'm a little younger than Caleb, in my late twenties." Kitty took a chip, dipping it into the salsa before eating it.

"What's Leo and Paul's deal?" Stacey asked.

Her closest friend was draped across the chair, drinking beer. None of them were drunk, not even close to being merry. The day spent at Lucy's had been a lot of fun. Cora enjoyed being around the club, even though James seemed to spend a lot of time watching everyone rather than joining in.

"You've made an impression on them. They've never had to chase after a woman before. It's novel to them," Kitty said.

"Tell me about it, it can drive you crazy with their egos," Teri said.

"So what's your deal?" Cora asked. "You're the chef at the diner, know the club. What's your deal?"

"Are you going to beat me up for having a past with the club?" Teri asked.

"Not at all. I'm not interested in who James *was* fucking, only who he is now." Cora took a chip for herself, keeping her gaze on Teri.

She knew Teri and James were close. She just didn't have a clue how close they actually were.

"They cost me my job in the city. When James came to Greater Falls, he opened the diner, offered me a job, and the chance for me to run the diner how I liked. I agreed, and we're here now. I've fucked James, and we're friends."

"What about the rest of the brothers?" Stacey asked.

"Yes, I've been with Leo and Paul. To be honest, they've surprised me. I've never known them to get to close to a woman before. They tend to keep women at arms' length. You must have a pussy made out of gold."

All of the women burst out laughing.

"Not of gold, believe me. I'd sell it to stop working."

"You love your job."

"I know I do, but history can get so damned depressing. I mean some of the kids love it, and I love their enthusiasm, but others can't grasp it. It's already happened. What's not to grasp? Sorry, loose mouth syndrome. My students are the best, even the difficult ones."

"The students who are struggling to grasp it may be trying to get more out of you. You're a hot teacher," Kitty said.

"That I am." Stacey winked at each of them. "So do all of the guys share a woman or is it just Leo and Paul?"

Cora looked toward Teri and Kitty as they shared a look.

"What?" Cora asked. "What is it?"

"It depends on the brothers. I've known them all to share at some point," Kitty said.

"I've heard of them all sharing, but not in one giant orgy of a free for all. They're not shy about fucking women in front of the club."

Cora stuck another chip into her mouth, thinking about what she'd learned. Was James afraid that would scare her? Was he worried about her running away?"

"He fuck you in front of his brothers?" Cora asked, directing her question at Teri.

"Yeah. I rarely got to a bed."

Standing up, Cora brushed her hands.

"Oh, I know that look," Stacey said, rolling off the chair. "We're going to the club."

"Why are we going to the club?"

"Because I don't want James to keep part of his life a secret from me. I'm not some frightened, immature, little girl. I'm a woman. I know my own mind, I know what I like, and what I don't." Cora moved toward the room. "I've just got to get dressed."

She wasn't surprised seconds later when Stacey walked into her room.

"What are we going for, leather skirt? Short dress? Nude?"

Cora looked through her wardrobe and pulled out a pale cream summer dress.

"You do realize with your blonde hair, you look like you should be selling cookies, right?"

"I know. I love the fabric against my skin." She'd never been into tight clothes, or leather. In the summer trying to remove leather from sweating skin was a nightmare, and if not done right, it hurt.

Quickly getting dressed, she urged Stacey downstairs.

"Wait, Cora."

She paused, looking at the concern in her friend's eyes. "What is it?"

"I'm worried."

"What about?"

"Leo and Paul, they're not looking for a good time, and I don't want to hurt them."

Tilting her head to the side, she pulled Stacey against her. "Not all men are like your asshole ex, Stace.

If you want to, give them a chance. If not, be clear with them, but don't give them false hope. It's not fair."

"Thank you. I knew I could count on you."

She hugged Stacey close before they made their way out of her house. Cora locked the door, and they piled into her car. She drove toward the clubhouse, and she saw Jerry and Drake on the door with a blonde each in their laps.

They looked surprised to see her.

"Ladies, can we help you?" Jerry asked.

"We're looking to party. I heard this is a good place to start." Cora spoke up.

Teri and Kitty were laughing along with Stacey. It was taking a lot of control not to burst out laughing herself.

"Go on in," Jerry said. "At your own risk."

Entering the clubhouse, Cora stopped to look around. There were many couples in different states of undress. Some of them paused when they spotted her little group.

"I'm going to get a drink," Teri said, breaking off.

"If he's not here, he'd be in the back," Kitty said.

"I want to go in the back," Stacey said.

Looking back at her friend, she made sure Stacey could handle it. Stacey was a lot like her. Some men liked to think of them as sweet and innocent. The truth was, they weren't. They lived life to the full, and they did it together.

Following after Kitty, they entered the back part of the club. She was surprised to see a lot more of the club mingling, including Leo, Paul, Damon, Sean, and Pixie. James was sitting at a table playing cards. There was no actual sex or spanking going on. The room was … tame.

Pixie spotted her first, and nudged James.

She didn't stop and moved toward the table. They were not in one of the booths, so she was able to get to James. Straddling his lap, she wrapped her arms around his neck.

He placed his cards on the table. She didn't know what Kitty or Stacey went and did. Her only focus was on the man in front of her.

"I missed you, a lot." She pressed her lips to his.

"I couldn't come and join you. I got the warning that it was a girly night."

"And so it was. You know on a girly night the girls, they talk about everything, and you know what I found out?" she asked.

His hands rested on her hips, holding her in place. "No, what have you learned?"

"That you hold out a lot on me. You're not a liar, yet you're not truthful. I can't be pissed because you're not lying about it. All you're doing is not talking about it, and that I don't like."

She started to work his jacket off his shoulders, next came his shirt, which she tugged up. Cora wasn't kind either as she did it. She sank her nails into his skin, and watched him wince a little. He made no move to stop her.

Eyes were on her from the men in the room. Kitty Cat and Stacey had disappeared off into the background.

James moved his hands up to the top of her dress and started to work the straps down her body. She began to gyrate her hips on his lap.

Cora felt the hard length of his cock pressing against her core, and she moaned wanting it deep within her pussy.

"What have I not told you about?"

"You keep me at arms' length and don't tell me

your secrets about the club. It's a good job I make friends easily. I wouldn't know you've got this whole new world without me."

"I don't want to scare you off."

"You think fucking me in front of your club will scare me off?" Cora asked.

This was invigorating. She'd not been this excited in a long time. With the eyes of his men on her, she wanted to make James the envy of the entire room. Over the past couple of days, and all of today, she'd noticed he kept mostly to himself when they were in the group. She'd seen him arguing with Pixie, and she'd overheard the brothers talking about his shock. None of the women picked James over Pixie. His scar terrified them.

James's scar didn't terrify her. She found it sexy, and beautiful, a testament to what he'd suffered.

Stepping away from him, she wiggled out of her innocent looking dress. She wasn't wearing a bra, and from the bulge in his pants, James was very happy about that. Biting her lip, she turned around, presenting him with her ass. Wiggling her butt, she removed the thong she was wearing.

"Fucking hell, James is one lucky bastard." One of the boys spoke up. She didn't know who, and she didn't care. This was all for James.

Kneeling down on the floor, she crawled toward him. As far as she was concerned, James was going to be the envy of every single man in this room.

She gripped his belt buckle, and with her gaze still on him, she began to reveal his rock hard cock. The moment he sprang free, he gave a relieved sigh. Gripping the length of his cock, she started to lick from the base up to the root, lavishing it with her mouth. He groaned out, finally sinking his fingers into her hair. She gazed up at him, and it was like his eyes glowed with arousal. He knew what he wanted, but he wasn't going to push her.

Taking the whole head of him into her mouth, she sucked him deep into her throat.

In the background, she heard their strangled cries. James was holding on to what little control he clearly had. He shook a little.

Searching his pocket, she found his condom. Releasing his cock, she tore into the packet, sliding the latex down his cock, before getting up. Straddling his waist, she slammed her lips down on his while he guided her down the length of his cock. She gasped without breaking the kiss she was taking.

****

The brothers were right, he was a lucky bastard. James found the entrance of her pussy, and guided her down over his cock. She gasped, and he took advantage by sliding his tongue into her mouth. Returning his grip to her hips, he slammed her down onto his cock. They both cried out together, not once breaking the kiss.

"Lucky bastard."

"That's fucking hot."

Pulling away from the kiss, he pushed some of the blonde strands out of her hair, and stared into her eyes. Her green depths were glinting at him. Cupping her cheek, James knew he didn't want to lose her, and that was completely fucking insane.

She sank her fingers into the flesh of his shoulders, as she began to fuck him in front of his club. Cora was about to make him the envy of so many club members, and for that, he was thankful to her.

It had been a long time since he'd been the envy of his men. He gripped her hips and slammed up inside her. When the angle wasn't enough, he picked her up, and dropped her on the table that had the cards and money on it. One of the boys pushed the coins out of the way so she didn't hurt herself when she lay flat on the surface.

The boys held the table in place, and James fucked her, leaning down to suck on her rock hard nipples. He couldn't wait to fuck her without a condom between them. Until then, he'd have to get used to the condom. It obscured all the feeling, and he wanted to feel what he'd done to her. Her creamy pussy was all his doing, not anyone else's. He owned her pussy.

Cora belonged to him.

She wrapped her legs around his waist and met each of his thrusts. He didn't stop even as she came apart underneath him. With the boys holding the table into place, Cora moved her fingers over her pussy, and began to stroke over her clit.

Only when she came a second time did James allow himself to push over the edge, coming within the condom. When it was over, he picked her up and rested on his chair. Cora wrapped her arms around him, and James shuffled toward the table. His brothers were already picking up the cards and the money, which was thrown into the center of the table. He ran his hands up and down her body, occasionally sucking her nipples into his mouth. James played a hand of cards, and Cora kissed his neck, and held onto him.

After a time, she climbed off his lap, and James removed the condom, taking the tissues Cora had given him to clean up the mess. There was a trash bin beside the table, and he placed his dick back into his pants. Cora pulled her dress on but sat on his lap. She made no move to leave him.

The boys played cards, and Cora pointed out certain numbers, playing with him against his brothers. When he'd won the jackpot in the center of the table, he took Cora's hand, and made his way toward his room. He took the main bedroom in the top part of the clubhouse, away from the bar and the diner.

"That was a good little show you put on tonight," he said, closing the door.

She lifted her dress over her head, turning to his bed. "You know, this is the first time you've brought me here," she said, sliding onto the bed. "Oh, wait, you didn't bring me here. I had to come and get you all by my little old self."

James chuckled, throwing his jacket onto a chair. He removed his jeans, and followed her onto the bed. Gripping her waist, he slid her underneath him, and nipped at her lips.

"What was tonight about?"

She started to trace over his ink on his chest. "I got talking to Teri and Kitty. You don't need to keep things about the club away from me, James."

"They shouldn't have been talking club business."

Cora smiled. "They weren't. I asked them questions about you, not the club. They told me a few things, and it made me wonder. Is the good, old, powerful James, the president of the Dirty Fuckers MC, afraid that I'll walk if something sounds a little too … dirty?"

Rolling onto his back, James stared up at the ceiling. "You're the first woman to come into the club, and fuck me like that," he said.

"Nah, you've got to have had plenty women do that."

"No, not one. Sure, I've seen some of the brothers have it done, and thought it was damn hot. My face is fucked, and for a lot of women, my dick's not enough for them."

Cora moved her fingers up to trace over his scar.

"I guess you weren't looking for the right women."

"Pixie brought you to the back room."

She chuckled. "Pixie didn't even have a look in."

James wasn't convinced.

"You don't believe me?"

"He's Pixie. All of the women eat out of the palm of his hand."

"Okay, I was at the bar watching Stacey get it on with Leo and Paul. Pixie started talking to me, and I talked with him. He pretty much asked me if I could handle something a little darker. I was intrigued. I had no intention of fucking Pixie, nor will I ever fuck Pixie. He's too much of a pretty boy."

"A pretty boy?" James asked.

"Pixie expects women to fall at his feet as if he's some king or God to women. I don't find that attractive. Never have, and I never will. I wasn't even turned on by Pixie. I was intrigued by what he was offering." She shrugged.

"What about me?"

"You do know you sound like a girl, right?" she asked.

He chuckled. "I do not."

"You sound like a girl, but that's all right. I won't hold it against you. When I saw you, I was even more intrigued. You stared at me as if you wanted to eat me, but there was this glint in your eye that told me you didn't exactly expect me to agree to be with you. How wrong you were."

James took her hand, pressing a kiss to the inside of her wrist. "I don't think I'm going to ever let you go."

"You can't let me go until I say so." She pushed him down to the bed, reaching over his bed to the small cabinet beside his bed. Cora grabbed a condom, tearing into it. She wriggled around so that her back was facing him.

He left her to slide the condom over his dick. When he felt her lips wrap around his cock, he kissed. He wasn't one to be outdone. Grabbing her hips, he pulled her up the bed until she was straddling his face. Her pussy was soaking. He didn't wait. Lifting up he took her clit into his mouth and sucked. She thrust down onto his face. Sliding two fingers inside her pussy, he watched his fingers sink into her tiny hole. She was so small, and she squeezed him tightly.

Gathering her cream onto his fingers, he worked them to her anus, spreading her natural lube all over her ass. She moaned around his cock. The sound sent vibrations down the whole of his shaft. He grunted out, tensing when a wave of arousal hit him that was so intense it had him close to the edge.

Spider, grandmas, decking, wood, peas, frogs.

When he finally gained control over his cock, he plunged his tongue into her pussy, working her anus and pussy at the same time. Her cream exploded on his tongue, and he wanted it all. James wanted her to come all in his mouth, and to swallow it down.

Cora pulled off his cock, and gasped. "Fuck, that feels so good."

He pressed a finger against her ass, and she pushed out. Sinking into her ass, he glided his tongue up through her slit, to curl around her clit. At the same time as he stroked over her clit, he added a second finger to her ass.

Cora took his cock back into her mouth, working him to the back of her throat. She began to thrust onto his fingers and tongue. James didn't let up, bringing her to a screaming orgasm that had her deep-throating his shaft. He cried out as her throat tightened around him, sucking.

When it was over, he didn't have time to think.

Cora slid the condom on his dick, moved down his body, took hold of his cock, and sat right on him.

He gripped her hips and began to slam inside her, going deep.

In that moment, James knew he would be a total asshole if he gave her up. He wanted her badly.

With his hands on her hips, he turned her to the bed, dragging her up onto her knees. He slammed inside her, taking over her. Cora cried out, begging for him not to stop. James didn't let up. Fucking her harder than ever before, he went deep, digging his fingers into her hips.

Within seconds he came, filling the condom once again. Collapsing over her, he wrapped an arm around her waist, holding her close.

"I'll sort you out soon," he said, promising her.

Cora giggled. "I came multiple times, baby. You don't need to sort me out."

She looked at him over her shoulder, and James laughed. "Are you staying here tonight?"

"Do you want me to stay here?"

"Yeah, I want you here."

"Then I guess I'm staying."

Chapter Eight

One month later

"How long has it been now?" Stacey asked, over lunch. Kids walked all around them, and Cora stared across the table at her best friend.

"How long has what been?"

"You and James going steady?"

Rolling her eyes, she took a sip of her milkshake. "How old are you?"

"I'm being serious."

"So am I. How old are you? We're 'going steady'? We're having some fun, and that's all you need to know." Picking up her burger, she saw Ryan come out of class with his head down. She frowned, wondering what was wrong with him. Hanging around James, she'd come to know Lucy and the kids really well.

"You've been with James a lot. You've been blowing me off," Stacey said. Her back was to Ryan.

"What about Leo and Paul? I thought you were dating them or something."

"I'm not dating anyone." Stacey wrinkled her nose.

Cora was about to open her mouth when she watched three of the jocks swarm around Ryan. She kept her gaze on him, and when she saw the tall one sucker-punch Ryan, she was out of her seat.

"Get Sharon now," she said, shouting to Stacey.

They caught the attention of passing students. Ryan and the three boys were oblivious to the attention they'd gained. She saw Ryan slam his fist in the other guy's face, but then he was held, and they all started to pound on him.

Cora kicked off her heels and ran over the

ground, pulling the kids off Ryan.

"Hey, get off. You're on school property, and we do not accept that." She shoved each of the boys off them.

They all went to hit her, but stopped when they saw it was not a fellow student. Cora wasn't a teacher, but she was the adult present.

"Miss Short," one of the guys said, trying to come across all nice. "Ryan was pushing his luck."

Stepping up to the man, she glared at him. "Don't even try to lie your way out of this, Stuart. Your ass is mine now. I saw everything."

"Not like he can do anything. He's a fucking pussy."

"Your father works in the state right?" Cora asked.

"Yeah."

"He does deals with the local MC?"

Stuart stayed silent, but he no longer looked smug.

"I take your silence to mean yes. Ryan's part of that MC. I think you need to think about that," Cora said.

Sharon came rushing out of the high school. "What is going on here?"

Cora filled Sharon in, and with the help of Stacey, they walked them to the principal's office.

Sitting at her desk with her arms folded, she kept her gaze on the boys. Sharon was inside her office with Stuart. Ryan was slumped on a chair with a shiner.

"Who do you think she'll call?" Stacey asked.

"Their parents."

"Lucy's working at the bank today. I bet James is going to come and handle it."

"Will you stop?" Cora asked. "We're grownups. Nothing is going on other than having some fun. What about that don't you get?"

"The part where you're looking happy, and you're pretty much dating."

They were talking quietly to each other.

Cora didn't want to put a label on what she and James had. The last thing she was going to tell Stacey was the fact she'd been cooking them dinner regularly. They were either at her place, or the club. One of her favorite things to do was fucking him, and for him to be the envy of most men in the club.

From what she'd heard, Leo and Paul were trying to capture Stacey's attention but had failed.

She and James also went on a couple of dates to the movies away from the club. It had been refreshing going out. He was always surprising her.

An hour later, four sets of parents arrived, and Cora wasn't surprised to see James tagging along with Lucy. Cora had called ahead to the bank to let Lucy know what had gone on. Stuart's father was dressed in a suit, and he shook James's hand as they entered.

Sharon came and escorted all of them into her room.

"Wow, that looked scary as shit," Stacey said.

"Shouldn't you be teaching?" Cora asked. Lunch had long since finished.

"Michael's taking over for me. I didn't finish lunch, and I went and snagged us these sandwiches from the cafeteria."

Cora was starving, and she didn't even argue with her friend. Sitting down, she unwrapped the egg salad roll and started eating.

"Tell me something," Stacey said.

"I'll tell you something if you tell me something," Cora said, striking up a deal.

"Okay, deal. Do you have feelings for James?"

Pausing in chewing her sandwich, Cora thought about it, really thought about. "Yes, I do."

"Really?"

Cora nodded. She did like James, had feelings for him, but she wasn't going to be ruled by her feelings. "He makes me happy, and he doesn't make me feel bad or guilty for what I like. I've never had that, not once."

It didn't matter what she wanted to do to him, or for him to do to her, James didn't judge her. He didn't treat her like some weird person for wanting sex, hot dirty sex.

"It's time for my question," Cora said, bringing the focus back to Stacey.

"I'm ready."

"What's going on with you, Leo, and Paul?"

Stacey let out a sigh. "I hate this game."

"This is not a game. I'm being serious here. What's going on? I answered your question. It's only fair that you answer mine."

Seconds passed while Stacey took a bite of her sandwich.

"They've asked if I would be willing to date them both," she said, slowly.

"And what did you say?"

"I told them they were both crazy. I'm not going to date even one man, certainly not two."

"Did you really say that?" Stacey was many things but mean wasn't one of them.

"No, I couldn't bring myself to hurt either of them. They're so nice, and I'm just not ready."

"You know they're not going to be like your ex." Cora never said his real name. There were times when Stacey couldn't handle hearing his name.

"I know. I'm just not ready to settle down with a couple of men I don't know anything about." Stacey ran fingers through her hair. "I never know what to expect from them. They're nice guys, and any woman would be crazy to tell them to suck it."

"You're going to tell them to suck it, right?"

"I don't know, Cora. I'm not ready. I've told them both that I'm not ready. I don't want to hurt them. What else should I say?" she asked. "It was only supposed to be a bit of fun."

"Nothing. There's nothing you can say." They finished eating their lunch, and Stacey left to go and finish teaching her class.

The parents and their students left, one after the other. James moved close to her while Lucy and Ryan waited.

"I'll be by tonight," he said. "I've got to take care of some business."

"If you don't want to come by, you don't have to," she said, not wanting him to feel obliged to come.

"I want to see you." He dropped a kiss to her lips. "Thank you for looking out for Ryan."

"I'd have looked out for any kid. I don't like it when they're all outnumbered."

"See you tonight."

"I'll shave my legs," she said.

One week she'd forgotten to shave her legs, and they'd ended up in a heap laughing about her furry legs. James gave her a wink, and she watched him go.

Grabbing a coffee for Sharon, she walked into the office. Her head was resting in her hands. Cora paused. It was the first time she'd seen Sharon look so broken.

"Are you all right?" she asked.

Sharon jerked up and wiped under her eyes. "Cora, hello, what is it?"

"Nothing. I brought you a coffee. I figured you'd need it after that."

"Thank you, and thank you for making sure those boys didn't beat the shit out of Ryan."

Cora was even more surprised. She couldn't recall a day when Sharon actually swore. "No problem."

"I hate dealing with parents. I love the kids, and I try to help them. This is so hard all the time."

"I know, I'm sorry." Cora placed the cup down, taking a seat in front of Sharon's desk. "How are you?"

"I'm fine."

Sharon had lost weight in the last month, and Cora was worried about her friend. "How are things with you and Thomas?" Cora asked.

"I don't know. It's as good as it can be I suppose."

Cora wanted to ask so many questions but kept her silence.

"Have you heard the rumors about him?" Sharon asked.

Glancing up at her boss, Cora nodded. "I've heard the rumors."

"The whole town has heard the rumors. Misty likes to spread those rumors, doesn't she?" Sharon said. She started wiping under her eyes. "Sorry, I shouldn't be talking about this."

"Are they true?" Cora asked.

"Are what true?"

"The rumors?" She looked up at Sharon to see the shock on her face. "I'm not going to pretend I've not heard the rumors, Sharon. I just wondered if they were true. Rumors, gossip, it's not all the truth. Thomas loves you."

"I know he does. It's just hard, you know. He says they're not true, and it's all lies. I don't know. Misty likes to call me, tell me exactly what he has done to her." Sharon's shoulders shook for a few seconds. Cora got off her chair, putting her arm around Sharon's shoulders.

"Hey, I'm here for you."

"Thank you, Cora."

She held her friend, wishing there was something she could do to help her. This wasn't something she could fix. This was between Sharon and Thomas. "Have you told Thomas what Misty is doing?"

"No. I don't want to bother him with it."

"Tell him. I'm sure he'd be even more pissed being kept in the dark. He loves you, honey. Trust him with this."

Sharon nodded. "I'll do that. I better get back to work. A school doesn't run itself."

Cora left her alone, and walked back to her desk. Misty worked at the beauty salon down the street.

Sending Stacey a text, Cora took her seat at her desk.

Cora: Do u want 2 get ur hair done?

Stacey: y?

Cora: Tell u l8r.

Stacey: Hate text talk. Sure.

Smiling, Cora had a brilliant idea to help Sharon out. After she'd seen Misty she was going to have a talk with Thomas. Sharon didn't know how to ask for help. Lucky for her, Cora didn't mind doing things without being asked for help.

****

James knocked on the state's main office door in the town. His secretary was sitting at her desk, sending them startled looks. He had Pixie, Caleb, Jerry, and Drake at his back.

"I don't think he's expecting you," the secretary said.

"You don't have to worry about anything, doll. He knows who we are," James said, entering the main room. He'd knocked just to give the guy a warning.

David was on the phone, and when he saw who was there, he ended the call.

"James, I wasn't expecting you today."

"I'm not here on business, David. I'm here to talk about your kid trying to beat the shit out of Ryan."

"We're talking to him. He's at home right now with his mother. I promise you, James, it won't happen again."

James took a seat, staring around the office with a few family photos, the certificates, and a few pieces of artwork.

His boys stood behind him.

"Ryan's going through a lot right now. He's growing up. His dad walked out, and so far shows no signs of coming back." James leaned forward grabbing a paperweight off the desk. It had a dolphin in the center and looked a little too girly. He frowned, holding it up.

"My daughter, Kirsty gave it to me. I'm not going to hurt my girl's feelings by refusing to take it," David said.

"I can see that." James threw it from one hand to the other. "You will talk to your boy about the shit he pulled today. I don't give a fuck what his reasons are. He keeps it up, when he's old enough, he'll take on the whole MC. Ryan belongs to us. He's part of us, you get me?"

"I get you, James. I've told you I'm not looking for trouble. I'm a businessman, and I'm good at it."

James happened to like David. The man was a nice guy, and he didn't try to fuck anyone out of their money. He didn't have a mistress waiting around in the wings. He was a family man to the core. James respected that, and it was one of the reasons why he did business with David.

"Good. I'll see you at the barbeque at the clubhouse," James said, getting up.

"Barbeque?"

"It's nearing summer, David. We're all settling down. The MC has shown to be a nice bunch of men. We're hosting a barbeque around the diner with a potluck theme. The locals get to pick and choose what they bring. It's going to be a get-together, an event, a mingling," James said. "Bring your wife and kids. Stuart will see what he's messing with more than a kind word."

They left the office. Pixie walked beside him as they walked down the main street. James was heading toward the mall. He wanted to pick Cora up a gift. In the time they'd been together he'd not given her anything, and she hadn't asked for anything material from him. Sure, she'd asked for him to fuck her in her yard, around the back of the diner, and his personal favorite, on his bike.

She was everything he'd wanted in a woman, and held no inhibitions with anything. He'd fucked her in front of his brothers, not caring what they thought about her. No one else had touched her, and she didn't invite anyone to come near her either.

"Do you think the barbeque will help?" Pixie asked.

"If anything it'll give the little bastard a warning not to mess with us. There's not a lot else we can do. I'm not going to beat the shit out of a teenager." James entered the mall. The rest of his brothers walked away, going to get what they wanted. He didn't know, and didn't care, what they were hunting for. James passed several stores aware of Pixie watching him. "What else do you want to say?" he asked.

"I want to apologize to you."

"What about?" James saw the lingerie store up

ahead. Stopping in the center of the mall, he gave Pixie his full attention.

"For Cora. I shouldn't have been a bastard about her, or made out she was mine. When I took her to the backroom that day, she hadn't shown any signs of wanting to be with me. I liked the look of her, wanted to fuck her."

James had believed Cora when she told him the truth. Hearing his brother say this didn't change his thoughts. "Cora told me this weeks ago. What are you getting at?"

"You're my brother, and what I said to you made me more than an asshole. I'm sorry. I don't know what came over me. I love you, James. You're my brother." Pixie pulled him in for a tight hug.

Giving Pixie a hug, James chuckled. "I bet that took you days to prepare."

"I've been wanting to talk to you for days. Jerry told me not to fuck it up. All the brothers told me I was being an asshole. I didn't need them to tell me what I was doing wrong. I already knew I was being an asshole, but I just couldn't stop it." Pixie stared at the ground. "Forgiven?"

"I wasn't even pissed at you. Cora has told me she doesn't want to sleep with you. She's mine, Pixie. I mean that." He wasn't going to give her up.

"You're going to take her as your old lady?"

"Yeah, I am. I'm not going to come out and tell her straight away. She wouldn't like that. I've got to give her time to come around with the idea." He walked into the lingerie store, going toward the display of sheer lace, and assortment of colors.

Pixie whistled. "You really did win the jackpot with her, boss. She's a fucking star."

James smiled. He knew exactly what he'd won

with Cora. Picking up a negligee, he held it up. "Will I look good in this?" he asked, laughing.

One of the sales clerks came over. "Hello, gentlemen, is there anything any I can help you with?" She had red hair, and her cheeks were just the same color.

Pixie smiled at her. "Hey, darling, we're looking for his old lady. We can pick what we like."

"Okay, we have a discount today on all sheer lace. Let me know if you need any help."

She walked away, and James felt a little for her. The woman had seemed so damn nervous.

"Now, she'd be a woman I'd bend over and fuck all night long," Pixie said.

James glanced toward the redhead. She was a fuller woman, thicker thighs and hips. His brother looked interested in her.

"Go for it. She might be wanting a biker to blow her world."

"She'd certainly blow mine." Pixie left him alone to pick out Cora's gift.

His cell phone rang, and he was lifting up a red thong when he answered.

"Yep," he said.

"Hey, baby," Cora said.

Lowering the thong, James smiled. "Hey, baby."

"I'm going to be late tonight. Will seven be okay?" Cora asked.

"Sure, do I get to know why you're going to be late for me?"

"You know Sharon? The principal?" He gave a grunt letting her know he did. "Well, some vicious rumors have been spreading about her husband Thomas. I'm going to go and see if any of them are true."

"What are you going to do?" he asked, smiling.

She was a spitfire. Kitty Cat had grown to love her as a friend as much as the club had. She'd sucked them all in, showing them all love and attention.

"I'm going to find out if she's just being a bitch, or if there's any truth in it. I care about Sharon. She's my boss, but she's a good woman. I don't like to see good women getting screwed over. I never have, and I never will. Do you think you can wait around for me?" Cora asked.

"Sure. If you want I can go ahead and make dinner."

"Okay. Stop by the school and I'll give you the key. Take care, love you, bye."

Cora hung up the phone, and James stared at his cell.

"Love you." He spoke aloud, and not entirely sure why he did.

Love you.

Love you.

Love you.

Over and over the two words went around his head, driving him insane. She didn't love him. Crap, he pushed the words to the back of his mind.

You love her as well, you fucking idiot.

James picked up several of the negligees and took them to the counter. The redhead was trying to work with Pixie flirting with her. Her face was a deep red like a ripe strawberry.

"Would you gift-wrap these for me?" James asked.

"Yes."

"We've got to head to the school. I need to pick up the key."

"No problem. Suzy, will you give me that date?" Pixie asked.

"I'm sorry, sir, we don't date customers." Suzy didn't look up from her work.

James waited, pulling out his card when it was time to pay. He didn't say anything to his brothers as he drove back to the school. The moment Cora spotted him, she nibbled her lip and looked so damn petrified. James made a decision quickly. Closing the distance between them, he slammed his lips down on hers, taking the keys from her grip.

"Love you, too," he said.

He didn't give her a chance to talk to him. James was already out of the door.

Chapter Nine

Love you, too.
Love you, too.
Love you, too.

"What are we doing again?" Stacey asked, pulling Cora out of her thoughts.

"What?" Cora asked. The moment she'd said "love you" to James, she'd been panicking. The words had been natural. They'd slipped out of her mouth of their own accord. What had surprised her was his response. That kiss had been pussy meltingly good. She'd never been kissed like that with so much possession, and love.

"Why are we going to get our hair done?" Stacey asked.

"Oh, I talked with Sharon today. She's suffering, poor woman. You know I like Sharon. I don't want her to be hurt by anyone. Misty has been spreading these awful rumors, and I want to know if they're true or not. I don't think they are."

Stacey let out a sigh. "It really does suck. I like Sharon as well. She doesn't deserve to be treated the way Misty is."

"She's always wanted Thomas. In the last three years I've been in town, she's always tried to get Thomas. It's not fair, and I for one won't stand for it. It's wrong." Cora tapped her fingers on the steering wheel.

"You know Misty's a bitch, right?" Stacey asked. "She'll lie about everything."

"Yeah, I know. We're going to persuade her in our good old fashioned way," Cora said.

"Well, well, well, you want us to kick her ass?"

Cora had watched Sharon deteriorate in the last month. If Misty was calling her and talking shit, she wanted to know about it, and to put a stop to it. She wouldn't stand by and let anyone get fucked over by another person. Misty would tell the truth, and if Cora had to press just a little harder, she would.

Cora parked her car around the back in the parking bay for the beauty salon. Entering the shop, Stacey booked them in, and Cora saw Misty immediately. She'd made sure to book her appointment for when Misty was working.

The woman was wearing a tight little mini skirt, bending over and showing the world her ass.

Cora didn't like her. Biting her lip, she took a seat.

Fanny, the woman who owned the shop, came over. "Cora, it's so good to see you. It has been a lifetime. What's happening with you?" Fanny asked.

Hugging the other woman, she gave her a smile. Cora liked Fanny. She was a nice woman, a kind woman.

"I want to get to the bottom of some rumors," Cora said.

She'd grown up in Greater Falls, and when she'd come back to handle her father's affairs, she'd been greeted with open arms. The locals loved and had missed her. She was really hoping to work on that, in the next couple of hours.

"I don't want any trouble," Fanny said.

"I'm not going to cause trouble, Fanny. I want the truth, and that woman could be destroying a perfectly good marriage. I'm not going to let that happen."

Fanny sighed. "Okay, come on, let's get you started."

Stacey and Cora were handled by two other women while Misty was throwing out one of her vicious lies again.

"I tell you, I don't know why he's still married to

that woman. He's always coming to my place for a little of this, you know what I mean," Misty said.

"Who's that?" Cora asked.

Some of the customers looked bored with Misty talking, others looked ill, and some were lapping up the gossip.

"What?" Misty asked.

"Who are you talking about?"

"Oh, Thomas Redman. He's a sexy, hot guy. The local builder around here, and fixer upper."

Cora nodded. She glanced at Fanny, and her friend simply raised a brow. She was good to go.

"He's married, isn't he?" Cora asked.

The clients were all listening, and the beauticians were working along in silence. It would seem Misty wasn't a well-liked woman.

"It doesn't stop my man. He's going to leave that fucking bitch soon, anyway. She's nothing to him. He told me so."

Cora started laughing. "Yeah, right."

"What do you say?"

"Well, I came to get my hair done and here I am getting told some made up story. Thomas wouldn't look at you when he has Sharon, believe me, I've seen him."

"Honey, you've not even been at my home."

"Where's your home?" Cora asked.

Misty told her an address, and Cora burst out laughing. This bitch was busted. She'd passed that exact apartment building last night with James. She should have recognized Misty, and now she was so damn happy.

"Oh, my God, you lying little bitch," Cora said.

"I'm not lying."

"I happen to have been on the back of a bike last night," Cora said, looking at the women. "Was Thomas Redman supposed to have been with her last night, around nine?" Cora asked.

They all nodded.

"Well, James and I stopped right outside of the apartment building. I needed to stretch my legs, and I saw you, Misty. I saw you with a man who is the same height as you with long hair in dreadlocks, and that wasn't Thomas. Thomas is over six foot five, and has blond hair. That wasn't the man you were making out with last night." Cora spun in her chair, facing Misty. Fanny hadn't even gotten to the scissors to cut her hair. "You're lying, and you've been lying about Thomas, Sharon's husband."

Misty's face was red as she stared at her. "You don't know what you're talking about."

Cora stepped out of her chair and moved toward Misty. "No, you don't get what I'm saying to you. Keep spreading your lies, and phoning Sharon with these vile words, and I will make you pay."

"What will you do?"

There were ways for dealing with women like her. Calling her out on her bullshit, and all it took was talking to the right people. There were enough people who'd witnessed Misty at the time of her lies, so there would be people willing to speak up.

"It's not just her, it's me," Stacey said, standing up.

"And me." This was from Fanny.

Several women stood.

Turning to Misty, Cora glared. "Test me, Misty, you won't win."

"Misty, clear out your station. I don't want your vileness spreading through my business. I had no problems you talking about yourself, but when that is lies, and it's directed at a friend of mine, I don't want to hear it. Get out," Fanny said.

Sitting back down, Cora stared at her reflection. She was shaking she was so mad at the bitch. How dare Misty be a bitch to Sharon?

Once she finished her hair, and had a facial, she took Stacey home, and entered the diner where she'd asked Thomas to meet her.

He didn't look much better than Sharon.

Taking a coffee, she moved to sit opposite him. "Hey," she said.

"Hey, I was surprised to get your phone call. I've been getting a lot of shit from the locals just lately. It doesn't seem to matter what I do or say. They all have their own thoughts on what is going on," he said.

"This over the Misty scandal?"

"Yeah, it's over that. I don't even know where it fucking came from. I don't go near the bitch. I've never touched her, and yet I've got everyone telling me what a bastard I am."

Reaching over the table, she held onto his hand. "There's something I need to tell you, and I don't want you to get angry."

"I'm curious. What could you possibly say to me that would make me angry?" he asked.

She told him everything, that Misty had been calling Sharon regularly, the kind of lies she'd been saying. All of it, and she didn't leave a thing out.

By the time she finished Thomas looked like he was ready to explode. "That fucking whore. She almost ruined my marriage. Do you know how close Sharon has come to leaving me? Fuck, this is a fucking nightmare. Before I realized Sharon was the woman for me, I didn't have the best reputation. I had no respect for women. Being with her, it changed me, and Sharon had to put up with what I did before her."

"I'm sure Sharon's heard the news of Misty's

confession."

"You saw her? You saw Misty with a guy she claimed to be me?"

"I did, and I know it's all lies. I care about Sharon. I don't want to see her hurt, not by you or anyone. I know your marriage is none of my business, and I'm not going to pass on anymore judgement on you. Talk to Sharon. You've got to be able to handle this." Cora finished her coffee, and stood. "I've got to go home. I've got a date of my own."

"What do I do? Everything is strained with us."

Sitting back down, she took his hand. "What do you mean?"

"Sharon and I, we were voted the couple that was not likely to make it. It's fucking stupid, I know, but Sharon has always been bothered about it. I couldn't give a fuck what others think. I love her. How do we get past this?" he asked.

"You take it one day at a time, one step at a time. Like I said, Thomas, I don't know what's happened in your marriage. Talk to her if you haven't already, or get her to talk to you?"

Thomas looked nervous.

"What?" Cora asked.

"We hit a hard place a year or so back. I wasn't the best guy to be around, and I may have said some shit that I didn't mean." Thomas said. "You know, Sharon never actually accused me of cheating on her. The rumors were there, and she didn't say anything to me. I was hoping she would, or at least laugh it off. She said nothing, and distanced herself, and I got so angry with her."

"Thomas, I've never been married. I like Sharon. I know her through work and seeing her a little here and there. I'd say the biggest problem is the fact neither of you have talked to each other. Nothing can be resolved unless you find some way to talk." Cora tapped his hand. She didn't want to know exactly what had happened, and she didn't want to know. This was between Sharon and Thomas. "I really need to go."

She nodded toward Teri before climbing into her car. Cora was home within twenty minutes, and when she walked into her home, the scent of steak hit her.

Her stomach rumbled, and she made her way toward the kitchen.

"Hey, baby, have you been keeping out of trouble?" James asked. He was standing at her stove, over the griddle where the steaks were.

"I'm fine, and yes, I think I may have helped Sharon and Thomas."

"You really do care about everyone, don't you?" he asked.

"I care about people who deserve it," she said. "Misty was being a bitch, and she could have messed up Sharon's marriage. I'm starving."

"Go and sit down. I'll bring everything through."

She took a seat, picking up her wine glass and taking a generous sip.

James came through with both of their plates. The steak looked damn good. He served it with garlic roasted potatoes and a salad.

"Does your club know you make a salad?" she asked, smiling.

He chuckled. "No, not really."

Cora took a bite of the steak and moaned. "You're my hero."

"So, you love me," he said.

She looked up at him. "I, erm, I don't know what to say about that."

"You could answer truthfully," he said.

"You make me feel good," she said. "I like you, James. I like you a lot."

"I like you, too."

"I don't want this to change who we are."

"There's something I've not told you, Cora. I want you to listen to me, so hear me out."

She nodded, picking up her wine.

"I like you, too. I do love you. I don't do marriage, but for you, I'd be willing to do it to have you as mine." Her eyes grew wide at his confession. "I like to have sex in front of the club. I've told you that, but what you don't know is the fact that I love to share my women."

"Share?"

"I like to watch my woman come apart in the arms of another man. I'm not talking about being out of the room, and watching through the window. I like to be part of it as well."

Cora bit her lip. Kitty and Teri had told her this. She'd been waiting for him to come out and say it.

Was she ready for this?

****

Two weeks later

James stood outside of the diner with the rest of his brothers watching the locals mingle together. The barbeque was being fired up, but he wasn't watching anyone but Cora. She stood on the edge of the group chatting with Caleb and Kitty.

They'd not broached the subject he'd brought up to her a couple of weeks ago. She'd asked many questions on the night about his need to share, and he'd answered them truthfully.

"How are you?" Stacey asked, cutting through his eye line.

"I'm fine. Are you going to keep Leo and Paul on

tenterhooks?" he asked.

"Aw, are you worried about them?" Stacey glanced over her shoulder toward Cora. "You know she loves you, right?"

He turned his gaze back to Stacey, frowning.

"Look, I know you and I don't talk, and I don't have a problem with that. You're not really my cup of tea. Anyway, Cora, she's been different with you in her life. She's never really been the settling kind of girl. With you, she's happy. I've never seen her this happy before in her life."

"I don't do marriage," James said.

"Neither does she. Cora wouldn't thank you for a wedding ring."

"Why hasn't it ever worked with anyone else?" he asked, and hating himself for doing it.

Stacey chuckled. "I see you've got it bad. Cora's a wild woman. She doesn't like to be told what to do, and how to do it. The men she dated took one look at the sweet ass dresses she wore, and her blonde hair, and believed she was the nice girl. Believe me, I had to sit and listen to them all talk about taking her home to Mom. Anyway, as you know, Cora isn't the kind of woman you take home to Mom. She's wild. She likes adventure. You're giving her that. You don't make her go around in boring ass suits, or wear tight leather skirts."

He looked to where Cora was standing. She wore a white summer dress with slender straps. Even this far away he saw she wasn't wearing a bra. The dress was sheer in the sun, and it showed she was wearing a nice white thong.

They didn't look like a couple, but he'd come to learn in the time that he'd known her that she loved the feel of the fabric of her clothes. She hated leather, even though she enjoyed wearing a leather jacket.

James had decided that he couldn't give her a ring, but he could give her something else to make her his.

"This life isn't for everyone," James said.

"I don't see Cora running away, nor is she trying to pull away from you."

He watched as she gave Caleb a hug. Turning her smile to Kitty, she embraced the woman as well. When her gaze landed on him, everything else just stopped. The only person who mattered to him with her gaze on him was Cora. She made her way through the crowd, nodding and smiling at everyone as she passed.

Once she cleared the path, she jumped into his arms, wrapping hers around his neck. "Hello, lover boy," she said, pressing a kiss to his lips.

"Hello, baby." He gripped her ass, pulling her tight against him. This he could handle for the rest of his life. "How are you feeling?"

"I'm feeling good. I've got a little surprise for you later."

James frowned. "I don't need you to get me anything."

"This after you spent hundreds of dollars on fancy lingerie for me?"

He shrugged. "That was entirely for my own benefit."

She kissed his lips, smiling. "Believe me, James, you're going to like this gift." She glanced across the parking lot, and he spotted Sharon and Thomas pulling up. Thomas climbed out of the truck, rushing toward his wife's side. Sharon, however, was already climbing out. He watched as Cora wrapped her arms around Sharon. Thomas took the pot that his woman was carrying, and moved toward him.

"How are you?" James asked.

He'd used Thomas's services on the diner, the bar, and the club. The man was a fantastic builder, and a great man.

Thomas glanced behind him, looking at his woman.

"I'll be okay soon, I think. I've got a lot of shit to make up for."

"Soon?"

"Yeah, some vile shit has been going on in my life, and I didn't help matters. It was like Misty knew we were in a bad place when she started spewing lies. I swear if I ever am alone with Misty, I'll fucking kill her." Thomas looked toward his wife, who was talking with Cora. "I fucking love her, man. I wouldn't touch another woman even if they fucking begged me to."

James slapped him on the back. "I know what you mean." He stared at Cora. "Since I've had Cora, there hasn't been anyone else. I don't want anyone else."

"Are you going to marry her?"

"Nah, I don't believe in marriage. She's not the kind of woman who'll appreciate a ring." James had been thinking long and hard about the best way to get his wildcat on his side.

"Sharon had told me it was serious with you."

"It is. How did you end up with a girl like Sharon?" James asked, intrigued. Sharon and Thomas were the classic good girl meets bad boy from the wrong side of the tracks.

"I couldn't live without her. I woke up thinking about her, and I went to sleep thinking about her. Most of my life was spent endlessly moving from one bitch to another. Sharon's not a bitch. She's mine, and that was how I wanted to keep her."

Those words were exactly how he felt about Cora.

The rest of the barbeque went by without a hitch. He made sure Stuart and Ryan were known to each other, and that Ryan was part of the MC.

There wouldn't be any fights anytime soon, which James was happy about. He was getting tired of being called to the school. The only consolation he got out of being called to the school was the fact he got to see his woman.

Later that night, Cora took his hand, and led the way up to his bedroom.

"Am I going to get my surprise now?" he asked.

"You're going to get your surprise, and you're going to love it."

Gripping her ass outside of his bedroom, he pressed her against the wall. "I love you, Cora." Sliding his hand up her body, he gripped her tit in his palm, kneading the soft flesh.

She gasped, pressing back against him. He cupped her face, taking the kiss he'd been wanting. Pressing his tongue, he made love to her mouth.

"I love you, too, James," she said.

"You're my present." He pulled her hair out of the way and kissed the back of her neck. "This is all the gift I need." Gripping her ass, he cupped the soft flesh, wanting to be inside her, fucking her.

Cora pulled out of his arms. "Come inside."

James followed her, kicking his door closed.

She turned him around so that he had his back to the bed.

"Now, I've been paying a lot of attention to you, James. We're exclusive, in a relationship together, and there isn't going to be anyone else," Cora said.

They'd talked a lot about what they expected from each other. He didn't want Cora if she was fucking multiple men. If they were going to have any kind of fun, then this was how it was going to be. They were together, not with anyone else. He was more than happy with that.

"Now, you told me something the other day, and I've been thinking about it. I don't want either of us to be afraid to admit what we want. I know what I like inside and outside of the bedroom." She tugged her shirt from her body and threw it to the floor. "I know what you want from me, but you're afraid of asking. You don't need to be afraid about what you want."

There was a knock at his bedroom door. James tensed, but Cora smiled.

He watched her walk to the door.

"Come on in," she said.

Caleb walked through the door.

James stared from Caleb to Cora, and realization hit him. She was giving him the green light to share her.

The door was closed once again, and Cora stepped up to him.

"You like sharing me, but I refuse to fuck your brother Pixie. I've done a lot of thinking about it, and I'm not going to fuck your brother. I know he's the one you share all your women with, but I'm not going to be shared by him. I want you, James. I'm not attracted to Pixie. I don't want him."

He cupped her cheek. "I wasn't going to share with Pixie. I was going to ask Caleb when you were ready."

She kissed the inside of his wrist. "I'm ready, baby. If this is what you want, then take it. I'm here, and I'm yours for the taking." She went on her toes, and pressed her lips against his. He was turned on, and out of the corner of his eye, he saw Caleb lean against the wall. It was fucking hot having an audience and to know he was going to be sharing her pleasure with another man.

He wasn't interested in touching Caleb, but he

couldn't wait to watch her go up in flames between them.

"She came to me, James. If you don't want me to be here, I'll go," Caleb said.

Looking from Cora to Caleb, then back again, he smiled. "I've not got a problem with this." He tugged his shirt over his head, and pointed at Cora. "Come here, beautiful."

The night was still young.

Chapter Ten

Cora ran her hand up James's chest. He was so damn hard and muscular. Glancing down at his pants, she smiled. His dick was pressing against the front of his pants. Licking her lips, she lowered herself to the floor.

"You know I'm going to be the envy of every single guy in the club," Caleb said.

"She picked you. That's all I care about. I was going to pick you as well."

Staring up at him, Cora kept her gaze on him, trying to let him know she wanted him, only him. This was all for him. She found Caleb attractive, but that was it, and the idea of being shared with James was hot.

He cupped her cheek, and she didn't look away even as she started to open his belt buckle. The sound of the metal clanging together echoed around the room.

"You only share her with me. If I'm not in the room you don't touch her, understand? You're allowed to talk to her, nothing else."

"She's your property, James. I've got that. I wouldn't do anything to break your trust."

She pulled out his dick, gripping him at the base, and licked the tip. He groaned, sinking his fingers into her hair and holding her in place.

"Fuck, baby. You know I love it when you tease my dick."

Sliding her tongue up and down his shaft, she got him nice and wet before flicking the tip. He was coated in pre-cum, and she swallowed what she could get.

She heard some rustling behind her, and when she looked back, she saw Caleb was getting naked. Going back to James's cock, she began to bob her head on his shaft, taking him to the back of her throat, and then pulling up.

He tugged on her hair, and she pulled off his cock.

Caleb stepped into view. With James's hand in her hair, she allowed him to guide her toward Caleb's cock. She wrapped her fingers around his length, looking up at the other man. He looked in pain from her touch alone, and she didn't stop. She began to masturbate him, going up and down the long hard shaft.

James released her hair, and his hands moved down her body, gripping her tits, pinching her nipples. He knelt behind her, kissing her neck. "He wants your lips wrapped around his dick."

She turned, and kissed James instead, licking her tongue along his bottom lip.

He kissed her deeply, and Cora continued to work Caleb's dick, moving up and down the root. Caleb groaned, thrusting against her hand.

James was the first one to break the kiss off, kissing down her neck, along her back, then around her front. She gasped out as he sucked her breast into his mouth. Flicking her tongue along the tiny little slit, she moved in a circle around the head of James's cock. Cora continued to work him over and over pumping her hand up and down.

She did the same to Caleb that she did to James, licking up and down the shaft before finally taking him in deep into her throat.

"Fuck, James, fuck, you're a lucky fucking bastard," Caleb said, hissing through his teeth.

Yes, James was a lucky bastard.

She worked Caleb's cock while James touched her body. It was so fucking hot that by the time James found her pussy, she was dripping wet.

"You're so wet, baby. You're in for a treat tonight," James said, whispering the words against her ear. He hadn't shaved that day, and the bristles brought out goosebumps across her skin.

Closing her eyes, she basked in the pleasure he was creating, working her body as she worked Caleb's body.

"It's time for us to taste this pussy," James said.

Releasing Caleb's cock, she stood up wrapping her arms around James's neck. He picked her up, carrying her toward the bed. She didn't get a chance to move, as James gripped her hips, aligned his cock to her entrance, and slammed in deep. She cried out at the pleasure. She'd gotten on the pill over two weeks ago, and while the doctor had told her after two weeks, she should be more than fine to have sex without a condom, he did also stress that the condom wasn't a hundred percent effective. Between her and James, she didn't think it would be a problem.

They would take care, together, of any consequences that came from their union. She didn't want to get married, and neither did he, but that didn't mean they wouldn't be together.

Caleb moved onto the bed in front of her. She took his cock back into her mouth as James started to pound inside her.

After several minutes passed, and Cora was so close to orgasm, James stopped, climbing off her. Caleb and James switched places, only Caleb didn't slam his cock inside her. He knelt down on the bed, flipped her over, and started to lick her pussy.

She glanced down moaning as he flicked her clit, sucking the nub into his mouth, and moved down to fuck into her pussy.

James pressed his cock to her lips. He tasted of the both of them, and she didn't mind. Opening her lips, she took him into her mouth. She cupped his balls, moaning as Caleb slid two fingers inside her pussy. He was working her clit as well. Both men had her surrounded. It was too much and yet not enough. She didn't know how to handle the pleasure, and it mounted.

Neither of them allowed her to go over the edge into heaven. They kept her there poised and at their mercy.

"Get a rubber," James said, pulling out of her mouth. She was picked up, and straddling James's waist. He slid inside her, going deep into her pussy. She cried out, groaning. "Caleb's going to be fucking your pussy. I'm going to be the one fucking this ass."

He slammed inside her several times, and she cried out, gripping his shoulders. His cock was rock hard, thrusting within her walls, and making her scream out with need. She hadn't been allowed to orgasm yet, and she didn't know how much she could stand.

James took control, slamming inside her while Caleb climbed onto the bed. He didn't just wait around for instructions. He kissed her neck, cupping her tits.

"She's perfect, isn't she?" James asked.

"Yes." Caleb pinched her nipples then cupped them, offering them up to James.

Caleb released the breast James hadn't taken into his mouth, and slid his hand down, sliding through her juices, touching her clit.

"Please let me come. I need to come."

James fucked up, gripping her hips to pull her down onto his cock. She kept begging, and finally James showed mercy, and told Caleb to let her fly.

Caleb pinched her clit, and with James fucking her, she came apart, squeezing his dick as she did.

"Yes, yes, yes," she said, speaking over and over again.

They held her throughout her orgasm, and she

closed her eyes, basking in their touch.

Finally, the pleasure ebbed away, and she collapsed in James's arms.

"Did you like that?" he asked.

"I loved it."

"Good. We're not done with you yet."

She released a sigh.

James pulled out of her pussy, and Caleb changed positions with him. It was James who held her in his arms, as he slid her down Caleb's cock. She trusted James and slowly took Caleb within her walls. He was long and thick like James.

She'd made sure he was wearing a condom before she took him within her body. Only James would ever get inside her without latex between them.

This was the next step of their relationship, a trust building between them that took it to the next level.

Holding onto Caleb's shoulders, she groaned as he went deep inside her.

James kissed her neck, gripping her hips. It was he that rode her on Caleb's cock, pumping her up and down his length.

Gritting her teeth, she hissed as Caleb leaned back, and used his thumb to tease her clit. She was still tender, and she couldn't help her jerky movements from his touch.

"You're so beautiful," James said. "Is her pussy nice and hot?"

"She's so fucking tight. I've never had such a tight pussy." Caleb ran his fingers up the lips of her pussy before stroking over her clit.

"Hold her for me," James said.

She followed James's movements as he climbed off the bed. He moved toward the cabinet near the door. He bent down, opened a drawer, and came out with a tube of lubrication.

Seconds later he came back to the bed, and Caleb moved her so she was over his body. He lifted his legs, opening her up.

James's slick fingers touched her anus, and she gasped. He was about to take her ass. Glancing behind her, she saw him slicking up his cock, getting himself ready to slide his cock deep into her ass.

"Do you want this?" he asked.

"Yes."

She'd been waiting for him to take her, and now she was finally going to get her wish.

****

Cora hadn't tensed up, and James couldn't believe how lucky he'd become to have such a fiery, wild woman in his life. She wasn't acting the part either. Cora loved sex as much as he did. She was wild, and he could handle wild. They were both bad to the bone, and he knew they were as good as married in that moment.

Sliding his fingers over her ass, he got her nice and slick before pressing his lubed cock to her ass. He pressed the tip within her ass and held onto her hips. She didn't fight him, and relaxed her ass for him to slide inside.

Caleb had paused in her pussy, and James slowly worked his cock inside her.

She gasped, and he tensed.

"Are you okay?"

"Yes, it has been a while," she said, moaning.

Kissing her neck, James stroked her body, relaxing her once again. He didn't want to hurt her.

Working the last few inches within her ass, James paused, and gave Caleb the signal not to move. He didn't want to hurt her. That was the last thing he wanted to do.

"How are you feeling?" he asked, seconds later.

"I'm okay." Cora moved her head so that he could kiss her lips. He cupped her face, and thrust his tongue into her mouth. "Please, James, I need to come," she said, begging him.

Chuckling, he nodded at Caleb, and they started out slow. Caleb pulled out, and James remained inside her. When Caleb started to work within her pussy, he slowly eased out. James didn't leave her ass, leaving the tip of his cock inside her.

They kept their movements slow, and only when Cora groaned, and started to beg them once again did they start to increase their movements, thrusting inside her over and over again.

Their movements never once lost their pace, and they both took her hard. James pounded inside her ass, holding onto her hips to the point that she would bruise.

"Fuck, James, I'm going to come," Caleb said.

"Please, please, please," Cora said, begging.

"Come, Caleb, and bring her off as well." James couldn't hold back much longer. Caleb cried out, seconds later Cora followed him, and her ass squeezed him tighter than ever before, setting off his own release.

It felt like hours passed, but it was in fact only seconds before they all collapsed to the bed. He and Caleb had turned Cora so that she was between them. Their cocks were still inside her but now getting softer with the passage of time.

"Wow," Cora said.

"I loved my surprise," James said, kissing her neck. "You can surprise me anytime you want."

Caleb left the bed giving them some privacy as he disappeared into the bathroom.

James pulled out of her ass, and she turned around to face him.

"Did you really like it?" she asked.

"Yes, I loved it."

"We need to have a shower," she said.

"We'll take one together when Caleb's done."

Cora touched his lips with the tips of her fingers. "I wouldn't let him touch me without you."

"I know, baby."

Her fingers moved down to his heart. "I've never felt like this before."

When she looked up at him, tears had filled her eyes.

"Cora, baby, what's the matter?"

"I'm scared."

"You've got nothing to be afraid of with me. I love you."

"I love you, too," she said. She tapped his chest. "What I'm about to ask you, I've never asked another man."

James paused, wondering what it could be.

"Would you like to move in with me?" she asked.

He frowned. "You've never asked a man that before?"

She chuckled. "No. Most guys expect marriage after moving in together. I told you, I don't agree with marriage."

"Why?" James asked. "Don't get me wrong, I don't mind that you don't want to get married. I've never seen much good come from it."

"I watched my mom and dad. They were in love, and when she died suddenly, it broke my dad. I was in high school, and he was never the same. I didn't want to ever be controlled like that. It scared me. Then the other extreme is Stacey. Her ex tried to control every single element of her life. I don't want to be controlled. I can handle love, and protection, not the other stuff."

James took her hand. "I don't need a wedding

band on your finger, or a certificate to make you mine."

"Are we boyfriend and girlfriend now?" she asked, giggling.

He laughed along with her. "We're something. Besides, we could never be married."

"Why?"

"Married couples don't have the kind of sex we do."

She rested her head on his chest, laughing.

"Do you want me to leave?" Caleb asked, smiling as he entered the room.

Cora left the decision up to him.

"I think we can have a lot more fun, don't you?" James raised his brow at Cora.

"It's your surprise. You can be the one who calls time to end it." She dropped a kiss to his lips, and walked into the bathroom.

"She's going to be your old lady?"

"Yeah, I've got the jacket ready to give her. I was thinking when the term ends in a couple of weeks, I'll pick her up with it."

"The boys will be riding out with you?"

"Of course. They'll be there to witness her at my back, and we'll ride through town." It was as good as a marriage ceremony to the club.

"Everyone likes her, even Kitty Cat."

"When are you going to face reality with Kitty Cat?" James asked.

Caleb took a seat on the bed. Kitty Cat had been with them for so long, and James had watched Caleb fall in love with her. Kitty's real name was in fact Katherine. She wouldn't respond to the name.

"I can't face the reality with her," Caleb said.

"You love her, and she loves you."

"No, she loves me like a friend she fucks, who

gives her what she needs. She doesn't love me. I can't face the reality right now that she'll never be mine, James."

Placing his hand on Caleb's shoulder, he nodded. "We're here for you, brother."

"I can't walk away from her. This way, we both get to live close together, and have some semblance of a life."

James left his brother alone, finding his woman in the shower. He climbed in behind her, wrapping his arms around her waist, and pulling her tight against him.

"Caleb's in love with Kitty?" Cora asked.

"You heard."

"I heard."

"Yeah."

"I'm sorry. Kitty's not interested in settling down."

"You really do like her, don't you?" James asked.

"Like her? If she had a dick, she'd be the one moving in with me."

He slapped her ass, and Cora yelped. "Don't even threaten shit like that."

She chuckled. "Like I said, she'd need to grow a cock, have lots of ink, and be called James."

She wrinkled her nose at him.

"You're a vixen."

"And you love me for it."

He took the soap from her hands and started to wash her body.

"So, what's in store for the Dirty Fuckers MC?" she asked.

They'd started talking about the club, and what the plans were for a long time.

"There are three buildings that can be bought, but I really don't have a clue what business to set up."

James picked up the shampoo washing her hair, and Cora moaned.

"I've been thinking about that and about the club. I've got an idea."

James washed her hair with the conditioner. "What would you recommend?"

"You're all from foster homes. Kitty told me how bad it was in one of the homes she was at."

"Yeah?"

"Why don't you open up a foster home? I know it's not a lucrative business, but you can't tell me that your investments aren't working out, and the diner? You've set up a successful business in Greater Falls, and I know you're the one who made the donations of the computers to the high school."

James cupped her cheek, and covered her lips with his. "You're a genius, you know that?"

"I don't think it'll be easy to set up, but if you and the boys want to work it, I can help."

"I like that idea. I'll run it by the boys, and then we'll move forward with what we'd need to do."

"You could help so many people, James."

"What makes you think I'm such a good person?" he asked, pressing her against the wall.

"Because I've spent a great deal of time watching you. I know you care about so many people. You love your brother to the point you're happy to be passed over. You love me, and you're prepared not to marry because I don't want it. The club is taken care of, and Teri got the diner because of the club. Do you want me to go on? You don't do drugs or guns. Sure, you know how to take care of yourself. Who doesn't? You like to fuck and drink? I don't see a problem with that."

James silenced her with a kiss. It was the only way to shut her up long enough.

Epilogue

One month later

"I think it's pretty amazing what they're doing," Sharon said.

Cora smiled over at her friend. She stood with Sharon, Stacey, and Ryan while they watched the students leave for the term. They had two weeks all to themselves. James had gotten the large house near the library, and the permission to look into fostering children. The club was going to be the main funders, and they were looking for someone to run the house. So far, the two people who had been the best options had been Caleb and Kitty, known as Katherine.

What Cora hadn't known at the time was Kitty had studied to be a caregiver, and was halfway through becoming a social worker. She stayed with the club and did most of her studies online.

"Me, too," Stacey said. "It's hard to get aroused anymore when you realize they're good guys."

Ryan shot her a glare and moved away.

"Oops, sorry, Ryan," Stacey said.

"You'll be suspended if you keep that up," Sharon said.

"Please, I can handle whatever a parent can throw at me."

Thomas pulled up in the parking lot, and ran toward Sharon. Cora watched the couple, and saw there was still some tension between them. She felt sorry for both Thomas and Sharon. They were two beautiful people, and yet they were struggling to find some happiness. She didn't know what happened behind closed doors, but that wasn't her problem.

"So how's married life?" Stacey asked.

Cora frowned when she saw that Stacey was looking at her. "What?"

"You heard me. You and James are pretty much married."

Rolling her eyes, she looked at the students leaving. "Shut up."

"Come on. You're practically married," Stacey said.

"We're very happy, actually." They had moved in together, and when they weren't at her place, they went to the club. She'd been shared with Caleb a couple of times, and each time was as hot as the last. Cora would do anything for James. She finally knew what it was like to be in love, and she could just about handle that.

The sound of bikes, a lot of bikes, coming toward the school met her ears. She turned away from her friend and moved toward Ryan.

"What's going on?" she asked.

"It's a surprise."

She looked down to find Ryan smiling.

Her heart was pounding, and she saw the club turn a corner, and ride toward the school. She licked her suddenly dry lips, and watched as they pulled up outside of the school. James was in the lead, and she stayed still as Ryan gripped her arm when she made to move toward him.

Staying still, she watched as James climbed off his bike, and moved toward her.

"What's goin—"

She didn't get to finish what she was saying as his lips were on hers, cutting off all of her words. She moaned, wrapping her arms around him, and he pulled her close.

Running her hands up his chest, Cora forgot about where they were, and cocked her leg over his hip.

Finally, James pulled away from her, and got down on one knee.

No, no, no, no.

She loved James with all of her heart, and she wanted to spend the rest of her life with him. She still didn't want to get married.

"I love you, Cora. This is not a wedding ring, or a marriage proposal. Get that look off your face."

She giggled and pressed her hand to her lips. They must look like a weird couple. She was wearing one of her pastel summer dresses while he was dressed in leather.

"You're my woman in all the ways it matters to me. I'm not going to change my own beliefs with you." He reached inside his jacket, and started to unfold another leather jacket. "I'm going to ask you to be my old lady, to ride at my back, and to be by my side. This is my version of a wedding band, Cora. This will make you my woman, and you can't leave, not ever."

She took the jacket from his fingers, and saw the words, "James's old lady" printed on the back, with the words, "Bad to the Bone", underneath the club insignia of "DFMC".

Running her hand over the patch, she smiled at James.

"You know how to surprise a woman."

"It means you'll be mine, have my kids if we decide to have any, and be mine always."

Tilting her head to the side, she glanced behind him at the club, then back at him.

"I take the right side of the bed?" she asked.

He burst out laughing, and Cora pulled the jacket on.

"You've got a deal, Prez."

"Come on, we're going for a ride," James said,

taking hold of her arm.

She gave Stacey, Sharon, Thomas, and Ryan a wave. Climbing on the back of James's bike, she wrapped her arms around his waist.

"Where are we going to go?" she asked.

"I don't give a fuck so long as you're the one at the back of my bike."

How romantic, and Cora wouldn't have it any other way.

The End

www.samcrescent.com

SAM CRESCENT

EVERNIGHT PUBLISHING ®

www.evernightpublishing.com